VIOLETTA ARMOUR

S'MORES CAN BE DEADLY

DANGEROUS PASTIMES SERIES BOOK TWO

BY VIOLETTA ARMOUR

Published by Gordian Books, an imprint of Winged Publications

Copyright © 2020 by Violetta Armour

All rights reserved. No part of this publication may be resold, reproduced, stored in a retrieval system, or transmitted in any form or by any means, electronic, mechanical, recording, or otherwise, without the prior written permission of the author. Piracy is illegal. Thank you for respecting the hard work of this author.

This is a work of fiction. All characters, names, dialogue, incidents, and places either are the product of the author's imagination or are used fictitiously. Any resemblance to actual events, locales, or people, living or dead, is entirely coincidental.

All rights reserved.

ISBN: 978-1-0881-6196-8

Dedication

This book is dedicated to all who were ever summer camp counselors.
To those who created a positive experience for children,
teaching them new skills,
but most importantly, building their self-esteem.

And to all the campers I was "Mom" to for three summers and especially my first
two little campers, Tim and Roberta who were ages five and four months.

History of Good Fellow Club Youth Camp.

Although the persons and events in this story are fictional, the actual Good Fellow Club Youth Camp location in north west Indiana was the inspiration for my setting.

From summers 1969 through 1971, my husband Bob Duffy, a coach at Wirt High School in Gary, Indiana, was asked to serve as Camp Director. He and I, along with our children, Tim (age 5)and Roberta (4 months) and a staff of twenty-four lived at the campsite for three adventurous summers.

The historic summer camp comprises 63 acres of rolling woodland along the Little Calumet River. It was built by the U.S. Steel Company for its employees' children. U.S. Steel's Gary Works Good Fellow Club operated the camp with its nine historic buildings from 1941 to 1976.

The National Park Service purchased the camp in 1977 for inclusion within the national lakeshore. Today it is the site of the Indiana Dunes Environmental Learning Center and the offices of the Great Lakes Research Center.

The Good Fellow Club Youth Camp was a short train ride from Gary, enabling workers' children to enjoy the environmental benefits of healthful recreational activities in the forest near Lake Michigan. The camp accommodated 60-100 children, ages 8-15. Children came for one-week segments.

U.S. engineers designed the camp and its layout using modern ideas available from publications like Architectural Digest. The team chose rustic log buildings to blend with the natural surroundings. The camp opened on July 20, 1941, and consisted of an administration building, a caretaker's cottage, 10 tent platforms, the washhouse and dispensary. New additions after the war in 1946 consisted of a stainless-steel swimming pool, tennis courts, a playground, shuffleboard, basketball courts, and archery range.

Camp staff and club sponsors wanted campers to learn values of sportsmanship, democratic living, proper etiquette, outdoor appreciation and spirituality during their week at camp. They emphasized the spirit of friendship that existed between early American pioneers and Indians. They embraced Native American Lore.

For further detailed information and history on the campsite and the mission of the Good Fellow Club, go to http://www.nps.gov/indu/History/goodfellow.htm

Revenge - A bitter desire to injure another for a wrong done.
Webster's Encyclopedic Unabridged Dictionary of the English Language:

-Revenge his foul and most unnatural murder
Hamlet. William Shakespeare.

You have heard that it was said, 'Eye for eye, and tooth for tooth.'
But I tell you, do not resist an evil person.
If anyone slaps you on the right cheek, turn to them the other cheek also.
New American Standard Bible Matthew 5:38-39

"It's a wonder I haven't abandoned all my ideals, they seem so absurd and impractical. Yet I cling to them because I still believe, in spite of everything, that people are truly good at heart."
The Diary of Anne Frank 1944

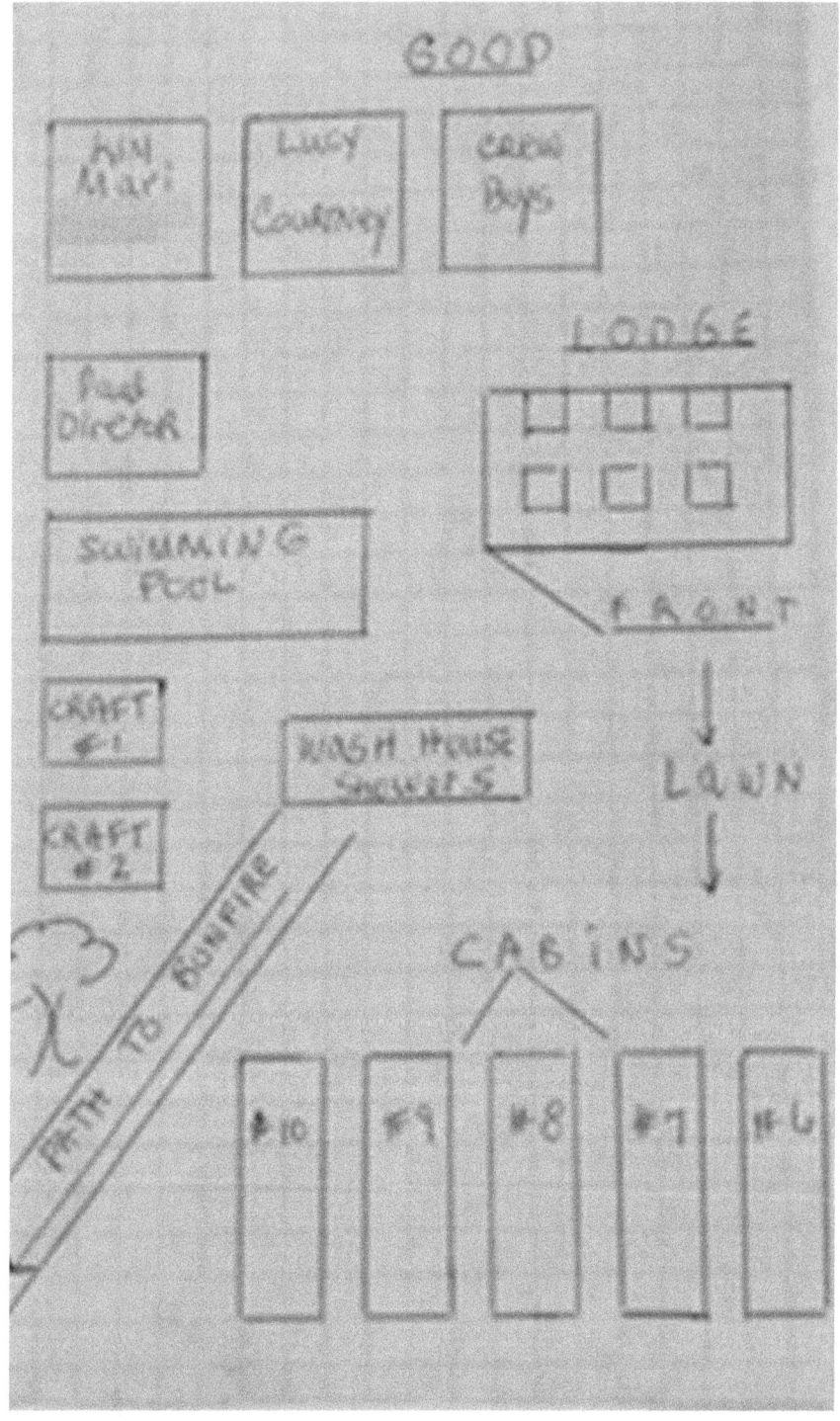

S'MORES CAN BE DEADLY

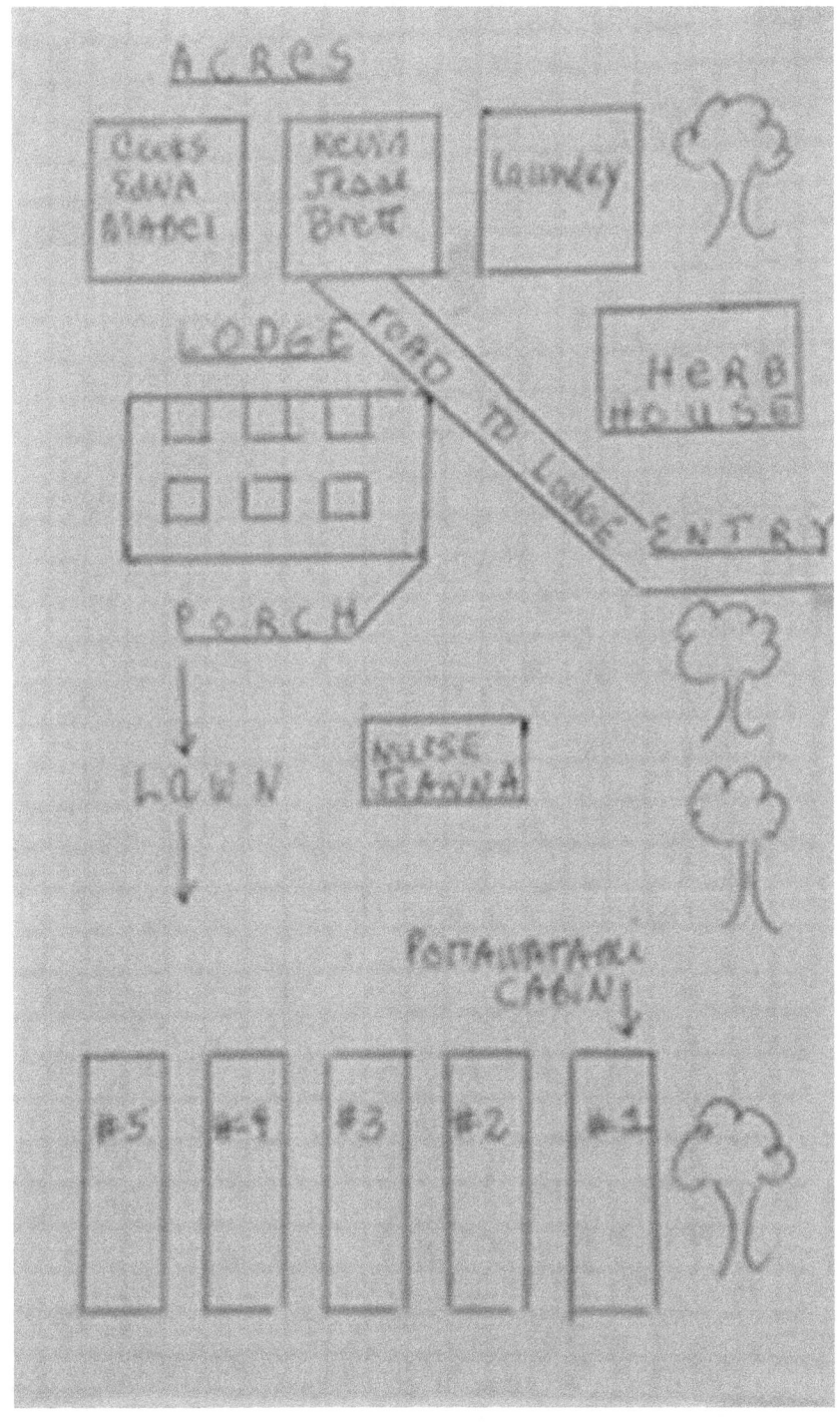

VIOLETTA ARMOUR

Prologue

The mailman trudged through a foot of snow to slip the envelope addressed to Kim Douglas into the mail slot that landed in her parents' foyer. Was it serendipitous that it arrived while she was visiting them in Indiana during the Christmas holiday?

The plain square crème-colored envelope appeared innocent enough. It looked, in fact, tasteful and inviting. The contents of the envelope would, however, set into motion a series of events that would change Kim's life forever.

VIOLETTA ARMOUR

December 2009
The Invitation

"**What rotten timing.**" I open the invitation to my fifteenth high-school class reunion, tugging at the waistband of my grey sweats—the sweats I bought in Wal-Mart's mens' department, no less, to disguise the thirty pounds I've gained since Mike walked out.

My mother waves the invitation in the air, as if it were a White House gala invitation—all part of the family's constant attempt to bolster my spirits. My first Christmas since the divorce.

My younger sister, Amy, peers over my shoulder. "Read it out loud," she says.

If you can't attend, please send an update for our reunion booklet. Whatever you'd like your classmates to know about you and your life today. Don't be modest. Be honest.

Oh sure, like I'm going to tell them my marriage has fallen apart. And that my company downsized while my closet upsized. Funny how fast you can go from a size six to sixteen when the man you thought you'd grow old with—when the one who said, "I do," didn't. Didn't keep his vow and couldn't even be original about it. Fell for the cute young secretary. And while he was chasing Bimbo Buns around her desk, I no longer had a desk. No desk, no title, no paycheck and nowhere to go on Monday morning. Or on a Saturday night.

"So, when is it?" Mom asks.

"End of May. Looks like Memorial Day weekend."

"That's some planning committee. Five months' notice," Amy says.

I continue reading. *Make your New Year's resolutions now to lose those ten pounds. Get in shape, dust off your dancing shoes, dig out your yearbook and join us for a night of dancing and reminiscing with the class of '95 at Jefferson High.*

"You're going to go, aren't you?" Amy asks.

The deadpan look I give her requires no words. Something along the lines of, "You've got to be kidding."

"You have to go. Prom queen, cheerleader. What's more, you have a social and moral obligation to show up." Amy is the cheerleader now.

"Oh, sure, like I want anyone to see me this way, especially Mike." I give the grey sweats another tug. To make matters worse, Mike and I were high-school sweethearts.

"My point exactly," Amy goes on. "The timing of this reunion is perfect. It's just the push you need. What are we talking here? Five months. Thirty pounds. You can do it, Kim. I know you when you set your mind to something."

Amy has put me on a pedestal all her life. Two years younger than me, she shadowed me throughout our growing-up years. Imprinting at an early age. When I started dating, she'd watch me wide-eyed as I applied lipstick, hoping I'd dot her lips with the latest shade of raspberry or plum.

"Sorry, Amy, this is one party you're not going to watch me play dress-up for. Especially if Mike brings BB," our nickname for Bimbo Buns. Or Big Boobs. Either name fit.

Amy ignores me. "Yes, I see a slinky red dress. Definitely your color. Size six. Something to knock his sorry eyes out. Everyone will be telling you how great you look, and Mike will have that silly teenager at his side who won't know a soul there. Come on, Kim. Fight back."

I don't respond as we continue to drink our coffee at the round kitchen oak table, scratched and scarred from many years of board games and spilled Kool-Aid. My mother's eyes dart between us like a tennis volley. She's witnessed many of these sister conversations at this very table.

I sit peering into my coffee cup like it holds the answers to the universe, avoiding their pleading eyes. Amy's words, "fight back" stir something in me. I know she's looked up to me all these years.

"I'll think about it," I say and walk to the sink and rinse out my cup. I climb the stairs to the dormer bedroom I grew up in and throw the invitation on the dresser top. Staring back at me are Mom's favorite photos of me: grade school, high school, college. She has tactfully removed the one of my wedding day and replaced it with a beach photo taken just a few years ago. Wisps of my sun-bleached hair are blowing across my face and my head is thrown back in a laugh. I remember the day it was taken. When did I last laugh like that—with wild abandon and joy?

On the floor are some scrapbooks Amy and I dug out, as we seem to do whenever we have an extended visit. One is open to the page showing all my Girl Scout badges. Ambitious with confidence, I had more than anyone in the troop. The other half of the page shows the awards from Good Acres summer camp. There's a group shot of ten girls grinning into the sun under the wood-burned Pottawatami sign above our cabin entrance.

I check on the bottom shelf of the bookcase where my high school yearbooks are stacked and pull out my senior year. Under my photo reads, Kim Douglas. Cheerleader, Prom Queen, Editor-in-Chief of school paper. Voted Most

Likely to Succeed.

I turn the page to Mike's photo but stop myself. No, he isn't in the picture anymore. I am through looking for Mike. I'm searching for the girl I used to be, the one who loved life.

I had it all, as predicted. It was a smooth ride on the fast track: college, marriage, career. Now total derailment. Like a train careening off a cliff.

I can feel my anger at Mike churning in me again, but I realize he has taken enough from me. I don't want him back. I want me back.

I grab the invitation, walk down the stairs where Mom and Amy are still sitting, munching on the Christmas cookies that typically sit on the lazy Susan on the center of the table till New Year's Day.

"Amy, you are so right. The pity party has gone on long enough."

My sister and mother peer up at me with what looks like anticipation.

"This invitation says May 29. Today's December 29. Five months to the day. It's a sign. I've got five months to turn my life around."

Amy jumps up and hugs me. Mom has tears in her eyes. I don't want everyone to get weepy so I keep ranting.

"And I'm starting right now." For emphasis I pound the oak table, almost knocking over the plate of cookies. Even four days after Christmas, they look pretty inviting. Then I picture the leftover turkey in the fridge and yummy late-night sandwiches slathered with mayo. A few potato chips on the side. Not those cardboard baked ones. The thin greasy ones with full fat grams from our hometown supplier. There's a pecan pie waiting to be polished off too.

"You know, guys, I don't want to fail at this, so I'd better have one last fling with this holiday food." I reach for my favorite, a snicker doodle. Then I take two, knowing their buttery taste will have to last me a long time. "I'll start January first like the rest of the world." I speak with confidence, but do I still have what it takes to be disciplined?

I wake up New Year's Day with a strong determination to succeed and an even stronger headache, reminding me that I should never drink champagne. At least not in the quantities I did when the family New Year's toasts began. We began with the usual health and happiness but soon deteriorated to the mundane and ridiculous.

To sunny days, to autumn days, to snowy days by the fire. You get the picture. Each toast required a healthy dose of the bubbly.

The only toast I need now is dry toast. A perfect start to my new eating plan. Five months-thirty pounds. No problem.

Of course, I have eaten enough the last two days to hibernate until spring.

January–May 2010
The Challenge

In the months that follow, I eat like a rabbit and run like one too. That is until my feet slip out from under me one icy Chicago morning. I finally fork over the bucks and join a gym and begin spin classes, palates, and water aerobics. Heck, I have all the time in the world with no job. The pounds are coming off the outside; inside I feel hollow. Unless you count the anger at Mike that fills my pores.

On the upside, my freelance writing is selling, and I land an assignment with a big advance. I realize this could be a decent career. No rush-hour traffic, no spending half a paycheck on lunch hours and pantyhose. No stress from ad agency deadlines and disgruntled clients.

On the downside, no friends at work, no celebrations after a successful ad campaign, no paycheck. I even miss complaining about the people at work who drove me crazy.

I take a one-night cooking class at Sur La Table. Seems crazy to focus on food while trying to lose weight, but it's all about low carbs. It's fun so I sign up for another six-week course. I learn a lot besides cooking. A few wonderful techniques that make me feel like a gourmet cook even if I'm not. Mostly women fill the class, one guy with his wife, and one gay guy. I keep telling myself I'm not here to meet men. I'm here to expand my interests but, in all honestly, I miss having friends. From work, from the couples Mike and I know. They now seem uncomfortable with just one of us.

Most of all I miss being married. Beside the loneliness, what I fear most is that my heart is a cold lump of lead. I'll never let anyone in again. How can I trust them with my feelings? Or trust myself to make a good decision?

May 2010
The Reunion

"Kim, is that you? Wow, you're looking even better than in high school."

I turn to see a nice-looking guy with no clue who he is. I glance at his lapel and silently thank the reunion committee for putting our senior pictures on our name tags.

"Paul. Paul Shrader. You're looking great yourself." Really great.

Paul was my biology lab partner. The one who kindly took the scalpel from my hand when I turned as green as the frog splayed out in front of us. A nerdy hero of sorts who said he'd do the cutting if I took the notes. A great trade-off.

"I couldn't have made it through biology without you," I say.

"All these years and all you think of when you see me are frogs? Worse yet, dead frogs." He reveals a smile that I don't remember having such charm. And those warm brown eyes? They must have been hiding behind the dark horn-rimmed glasses he wore that made him look like such a geek, usually with a piece of tape on the bridge of the nose. Both the tape and geek are absent now.

I smile back. "I guess that's what these reunions are all about. Reliving the agonies of high school."

"Couldn't have been much agony for someone as

popular as you."

"Oh yeah, I had my moments. Falling during cheering tryouts comes to mind."

"You were just going for the sympathy vote. I know you got mine when you jumped back up and finished. Most girls would have hidden under the bleachers after that."

Gosh, this guy is saying all the right things. I catch myself glancing at the hand that holds his glass for a wedding ring. None.

As if he can read my thoughts, he asks, "So, where's Mike? I heard you two married."

"I couldn't tell you where Mike is, but he's definitely not with me. Hasn't been for eight months now. He went through his mid-life crisis a little early." I shrug as if I don't care. "I don't know why he couldn't have just bought a BMW convertible. He opted for the younger girlfriend."

"I'm sorry." He sounds genuinely concerned.

"It's okay. You didn't know. Actually, I was hoping he'd show up tonight so I could flaunt my new-found confidence."

"Oh?"

"Well, I'm not sure I have it yet, but I'm doing that old 'fake it till you make it' thing."

"You don't have to fake anything. You look great. Mike's the loser here. What's that Paul Newman saying, 'Why go out for hamburger when you have steak at home?'"

I wouldn't mind sharing a T-bone with this guy. He's saying all the right things while looking like an ad in GQ. Sandy brown hair, cut short, nice clean look. Eyes the color of yummy caramel.

"So, how about you? Are there lots of little Paul's or Paula's running around your house? I'm sure you found a way to put that sex education we had in biology to good use."

"Nope. No kids, no wife. Sex? You might say I'm a late

bloomer."

Is he blushing? How cute. I say, "It's a wonder any of us tried sex after that movie in biology with the gross anatomy diagrams. Pictures you couldn't unsee, even if you tried."

Paul laughs. "Yeah, I remember that one. The intent was to make us celibate, but nothing much deters raging teen hormones."

My hormones are definitely coming alive for the first time in a long time. "So what do you do?" I ask. "No, let me guess. It's got to be something outdoors." Who else would have a tan in May? "Are you in construction?"

His sport-coat sleeves fit snug around his biceps. Maybe a personal trainer?

"Well, a little of both. Constructing young minds, building bodies. I'm a coach and phys ed teacher. In Phoenix. Valley of the Sun."

"So that explains the tan." I'm relieved to hear that, as the thought of a guy actually going to a tanning booth for a reunion is a bit much. I considered it, but I have a mission to achieve for no-show Mike. Now it doesn't matter that Mike isn't here, with Paul's brown eyes close enough to mine that I can see the gold specks in them.

"I do teach one other class. Promise you won't laugh if I tell you?"

"Promise."

"Biology."

Of course, I laugh, almost spitting out the drink I've been sipping. "Couldn't get enough of those little froggies, huh?"

"Actually, couldn't get a job without something besides P.E. Big push for math and science."

Wow, brains and brawn.

"So, what are you doing?"

"I was a copy editor for an advertising agency in Chicago. Then the downturn in the economy hit hard. My company lost a couple of big accounts and I lost a steady paycheck."

"That dress doesn't look like something you got at a thrift store." The way he looks at me tells me that maybe Amy was right about the slinky red dress.

"I'm freelancing. It's turned out pretty well, surprisingly. Gives me time to do other things." Who am I kidding? I have no life besides my writing.

"So, what do you do all summer? Teachers still have three months off?" I ask.

"Depends on the district. Lots of year-round schools now with mini breaks to break up the year. Coaching keeps me busy most of the year, but I actually have a great summer job for the next ten weeks. Right here in Indiana. My parents called me the minute they saw the ad. Any way to get out of Phoenix in the summer is a good thing."

"Oh?"

"They needed a camp director at Good Acres Camp."

"Good Acres! My favorite place in the world. I spent so many summers there. First as a camper, then as a counselor."

"Really? You liked writing your name in your underwear all those years?"

I try to respond with something clever, but the music drowns me out. They're playing songs from our era, Whitney Houston's, *Exhale*.

The oldies they're playing remind me of the dances in the high school gym. The only thing missing now is the scent of Old Spice shaving lotion and Heaven Scent perfume. I give a little laugh.

He gently cups his hand under my elbow and leans close to my ear. "It's warm in here. Let's step outside where we can cool off and you can tell me what's so funny."

I'm surprised at how good his hand feels. It shouldn't surprise me as I am surely starved for human touch. The first three months after Mike left, all I hugged was a tub of ice cream, and then it was weights at the gym. Neither of them hugged me back.

As we walk out, Mike asks, "So, what's the laugh about?"

"I was thinking of the time all the sophomore girls discovered rinsing our hair with vinegar gave it an extra shine. Nobody told us we'd smell like a dinner salad once we started perspiring at the dance."

He smiles at me like I'm the most interesting person he has met. It's been a while since anyone has made me feel this way. Step outside with him? At this point, I feel like I'd follow him anywhere.

We stroll into the courtyard and find a bench under a gas lamp, as far as we can get from the groups having a cigarette.

"Looks like high school all over," I say. "The bad kids smoking outside."

We each take a corner of the bench and put our drinks between us. The spring air is fragrant.

"You smell nice," he says.

"I'd like to take the credit, but it's probably the lilacs blooming."

"Oh yeah. No lilacs in Arizona. I'm going to enjoy a summer in the Midwest again. Now about Good Acres. Did you like it enough to perhaps do it again?"

"What? Go back to camp? I know I'm starting over, so to speak, but I don't have to go that far back."

"Here's the thing. I've got one hundred seven and eight-year-old girls showing up in one week. You must know the routine. A hundred kids a week for ten weeks. Five weeks girls, five weeks boys. One of my instructors just bailed out yesterday. Something about a free trip to Europe."

"Hm, let's see? Europe or Good Acres?" I hold up a finger for each option. "That probably wasn't too hard a decision. No offense to you."

"How about it? You can still do your writing."

True.

He keeps up the sales pitch. "In fact, think of all the articles you could write as the expert. "How to prepare Your Kid for a Great Camp Experience." And those girls will give you enough material to write a book. Harriet Potter Does Camp or something to that effect."

Remembering some of the pranks we played, I am inclined to agree. "So what position is it? What would I need to do?"

"Piece of cake. It's arts and crafts. I bet you're dying to make a lanyard after all these years. Who wouldn't love a summer playing in paints and beads? What do you say?"

"Sounds like fun, but I'm not into sharing a cabin with ten giggling girls. And for sure I'm not using that community wash house and bathroom that I remember. I know there's alternative life growing there."

"No problem. Instructors have their own cabin. You'll have a roommate, Mari, the swim coach. Teaches back in Michigan but comes every summer to visit her parents here. You two would have your own shower and bath. Indoors. And you get paid."

"Oh yeah, the pittance we made as counselors? Barely paid for our junk food. And to think we competed for the privilege."

"Okay, it's a token amount. But the good thing is you don't have anywhere to spend it. A built-in savings plan. Three free meals a day. The only place you can spend money is the canteen and the company store. You remember—sweatshirts, tee shirts, nighties. Anything they could put the Good Acres logo on." Then he adds with a sheepish smile. "By the way, the arts and crafts instructor is supposed to be in charge of the camp store at registration."

"Oh, great. this job description is expanding as we speak. Any other surprises? Clean out the pool every Saturday? Mow the south forty?"

He laughs, and I notice a little shaving nick on that nice square chin of his. I fight the urge to touch it.

He goes on, "You're off from noon Saturday till noon Sunday."

"So I can go into town and spend my big check, huh?"

"Or I could spend my check buying you dinner somewhere without a hundred kids." His smile makes me want to say yes immediately.

Somehow in the course of the conversation, we've edged closer together and under the gaslight, his caramel brown eyes have turned darker and soft like velvet. For some reason, they make me picture the narrow dark trail that leads the way to the closing bonfire celebration at Good Acres. It could be fun to do it one more time.

Because the camp was once sacred Indian grounds hundreds of years ago, all the campers wore the moccasins and head feathers they'd made on that last night. Campers walking quietly single file, their flashlights the only nod to the twentieth-century.

He must see me weakening. I don't let on, but when he mentions S'mores, I know I'm in.

"Now how many people have a chance to go back to their childhood? This is the chance of a lifetime," he says.

I smile at him. "I might be ready to take a chance."

As we walk back into the ballroom, I feel good. But what did I possibly commit to? Seeing this handsome hunk every day for the next ten weeks? I'm way too vulnerable right now. Am I opening myself up to more heartache?

On the other hand, camp was so much fun. Surely, it could be a great way to spend a summer.

VIOLETTA ARMOUR

Pottawatomi Cabin. Good Acres. Summer 1987
Dear Diary,

I don't like it here. The other girls make fun of me. I hear them chanting, "Pat, Pat, she's so fat. Made a dent in the bed where she sat."

I told Mama I didn't want to come. I don't see anything good about Good Acres.

When I walked back to our cabin from the wash house, they were all giggling. I peeked in the window and Trish was holding up a pair of my shorts.

"Oh, does anyone want to sleep in a tent tonight? I think these will be big enough to cover us."

Every cabin has a name for an Indian tribe. Ours is Pottawatomi. It's the Indian word for fire-keepers. When they make fun of me, I'd like to show them fire. I'd like to torch this whole place so I never have to come back.

VIOLETTA ARMOUR

Girl Talk

"Okay, I want all the details. Don't leave anything out," Amy says, pouring syrup over her tall stack of pancakes.

I spent the night at my parents' home after the reunion and meet Amy for breakfast the morning after at the pancake house around the corner. When our food arrives, I look with longing at Amy's plate as the syrup oozes over the melting pats of butter and then drizzles down the sides onto the bacon.

Although it has been many months, I recall the taste of bacon with a touch of maple syrup on it. But I am still basking in the good feeling of how my size six dress fit last night, so it isn't too hard to settle for two poached on whole wheat toast. I say the Weight Watchers mantra aloud after I order, "Nothing tastes as good as thin feels." Right.

"I'm proud of you, Kim. No bingeing on carbs after the big event," Amy says and stuffs a huge forkful of pancakes into her mouth. Even so, she manages to talk. "Well, I'm really disappointed that Mike didn't show so you could flaunt your new bod."

"You have to remember, I haven't seen Mike for over nine months. He never saw me after I gained the weight, so the size six wouldn't have impressed him. That's the size I was when he decided to chase Bimbo Buns."

"What is it with guys? Some are so faithful even though their wives have let themselves go. You took good care of yourself and he had a roving eye? How do you know which species you're getting? I guess that's why I haven't taken the plunge." She stuffs another mouthful in. "Okay, not that anyone has asked me to plunge, but the whole thing scares me."

"It scares me too. Can I ever trust anyone again. Mike just didn't seem the type to ever do that. He gave no signs of being a womanizer. Was I too naive or plain blind? Did I have my head in the sand or what? Be honest with me, Amy. Did you see it coming?"

"No, I didn't. Honest. And don't blame yourself. Mike's got a screw loose somewhere. He's never going to find anyone as nice as you. I mean you're the one who always talks to old people and little kids. And you never say no to a Girl Scout even if you just bought a bunch of boxes from the first one who asked you, and—"

"Okay, Amy, enough already. I know you're trying to make me feel better, but evidently those qualities hardly compete with a BB in some plunging neckline outfit."

"Some guys just like the challenge of someone fawning over them."

"We were way past the fawning stage, but I thought what we had was better. Now I'm doubting the whole male species. And myself. My judgement."

Amy looks like she wants to crawl across the booth to give me a hug. "Do you still think about him a lot? Are you still mad?"

"Heck, I don't know what I am. It comes and goes. First I'm hurt, then about the time I'm getting over it, I get really mad again. I still catch myself plotting ways to get revenge—to make him hurt the way I did and that's not good. That's not me. And it's not the me I want to be. What

I really want is not to think about it."

Amy looks perplexed. "So, you think about this revenge thing a lot?"

"No, it kind of creeps up on me and takes me by surprise. Like when I see a couple talking intimately like they're sharing a private joke. I miss that. Someone knowing what makes me laugh. It would be like if you suddenly went out of my life. No matter how many friends I have, no one could ever take your place, Amy. All the things you know about me that I don't have to explain. Losing that intimacy is what hurts. It's then that I want to strike back."

"Yes, I'd like to help you strike back. I want to strike him, personally—like a knee in the groin. That physical stuff is a great release."

I have to laugh. "Since when did you turn physical? You were always the pacifist."

"Well, some actions require strong measures. Eye for an eye and all that. Heck, it's even in the Bible. Can't be all bad." She wipes some syrup off the corner of her lip. "What you need to do is find a cool guy and a way to let Mike see you with him. Give him a taste of his own medicine."

"I might have found the first part of that equation. A cool guy."

"What? Where? You been holding out on me?"

"I was getting to it. He was at the reunion. Looking ten times better than he ever did in high school. And here's the best part. I'm going to live with him this summer."

"Oh my gosh, are you crazy? Well, I'm all for it. I mean if that's what it takes to get over Mike."

Amy assumes I'm "moving in" with the new guy and for a minute I let her believe it. It's too much fun to watch her eyes open as wide as the saucer her coffee cup is resting on.

"It's not exactly living together. I'll have my own cabin."

"Okay, girl, you're not making any sense now. What kind of cabin? Oh, it's a cruise. You're going on a cruise?"

"No, not that kind of cabin. Remember Good Acres?"

"Of course. Best summers of my life. Who could forget?" Amy bursts into one of our camp songs, and the two elderly ladies in the booth across give us a disapproving look. We both smile back and then have to suppress giggles as we did when we were eight and ten.

"He's the new camp director and wants me to fill in for an instructor who bailed last minute. I thought why not? Have computer, will travel. I surely have nowhere else to be, so why not spend the summer at camp with a nice guy? A very nice guy."

"I couldn't agree more." Amy's face lights up like our Christmas morning tree. "But don't you need an Internet connection to research your stuff?"

"Paul said he's got a high-speed connection in his office and one in the third floor of the Lodge for staff. Off limits to campers, of course. Not the same as having it at my fingertips, but it'll work. Probably the only change they've made at camp in the last twenty years."

"I can't believe Good Acres has Internet. A real connection with the outside world. That was the beauty of camp. It was so isolated. We didn't have a clue what was going on outside of our campgrounds. Never even missed a whole week without MTV. Gosh, what a great place that was. Any other changes?"

"I hope not. I was thinking a return to nature—a change of scenery—might be good for me. A little diversion. Fun and games before I try to get back in the real world. I've kind of been floundering, you know."

"But I thought you were doing great now. You look good and you said your freelance is paying well."

"Pays well, but I never meet anybody. I'm okay during

the day, but the evenings are a drag and the lonely weekends are driving me crazy. Why not be surrounded by a hundred kids night and day? As I recall, when I was a counselor, by the time Saturday rolled around, I was too tired to care if I had a date or not. I just wanted total silence till the new girls came roaring in on Sunday."

"And maybe this time you'll save some energy for Saturday nights with this nice guy? What's his name?"

"Paul. Paul Shrader. My biology lab partner, believe it or not. We did the frog thing together."

"You know what they say. You have to kiss a lot of frogs."

"Yeah. I wouldn't mind kissing this one. It's the first sign of any feelings I've had since Mike. I've just been kind of numb."

"Kim, this is great. It's going to be a great summer for you. Did you tell Mom and Dad?"

"No, you're the first to know. They already left for church by the time I woke up."

"Mom will probably begin baking you care packages today. She's still suffering from empty nest."

"They'll probably get a kick out of it. Maybe I'll have them come out to the campgrounds some night for old time's sake."

"Yeah, they loved that place. You know they were always the first parents there to pick us up on Saturday. They missed us more than they let on. But do you remember how once they got there, they were never in a hurry to leave? They'd sit in those big wooden chairs on the front porch and tell us to go say thank you to all the staff. They liked to hang around and watch the other kids get picked up."

"I agree. Except that one year when they were really late. Had to go to a funeral or something, and I was one of the last campers there. I didn't care. The later the better. They could have left me there for weeks. But it was the first time I saw how scared some of the kids got when their parents were late. Like, Are they ever coming to get me? By the time their parents showed, they were almost in tears. I swore I'd never do that if I had kids."

Then all of a sudden, I feel the anger arise at Mike again. It comes out of nowhere. This time it's the thought of kids. Kids. The ones we would never have. Did we wait too long? Would he have stayed if we had a little boy with Mike's blue eyes and dimpled chin? Would he have left him behind as easily as he left me?

"Hey, earth calling Kim. Where'd you go? You have that glazed look again."

"Oh, nothing. Just plotting ways to sterilize Mike so he can never have children. It's that revenge thing kicking in." I eye her plate. "Are you going to eat that last bit of bacon?" I don't wait for an answer as I reach across and stuff it in my mouth. It's hard to give up the thought of a family and bacon both.

Mom and Dad are elated about my summer plans. Now instead of being ninety minutes from them, I will be thirty minutes all summer, although my only time off is Saturday nights.

As I'm leaving, Mom says, "Oh, that reminds me. I've been meaning to ask if you knew that girl who died—strangely enough, from a snake bite of all things?"

"Oh? Who was that?"

"It is totally escaping me now. I put the newspaper article somewhere. I was going to ask if you knew her because her obituary said she had been a Good Acres camp counselor for years."

Mom shuffles through some papers on her kitchen desk. "Well, I'm sure it will turn up somewhere."

Indecision

By the time I drive back to my apartment in Chicago Sunday evening, second thoughts enter my mind. Why would I agree to such an outlandish idea? Ten weeks at summer camp? Getting caught up in a few nostalgic memories and succumbing to those brown eyes? How foolish. And falling for someone while on the rebound is the last thing I need. I'd be putty in his hands.

I glance at the writing area I set up in the corner of my living room. That's where I finally developed the discipline to write each day. Like clockwork, I sit down at my computer at 8:00 a.m. Take a mid-morning break at the gym. Write after lunch for two hours. Research in the afternoon. Because my social life is non-existent, I often write in the evenings. I'm making a decent living and even putting some money aside. Why do I want to rock the rowboat with a foolish notion that this summer escape could be fun?

But as I glance at the headlines on the May 30 Sunday paper scattered on my coffee table, maybe it would be a pleasant change to return to nature, away from all the grown-up negative news. *U.S. Manufacturing Contracts to lowest level since 2009. Home foreclosures on the rise. Bankruptcies and Unemployment Continue. Swine flu outbreak. Gulf oil spill biggest in history.*

As if my thoughts have projected across the state line,

my phone rings and Paul's voice comes across as wholesome and appealing as it was last night. I now remember why I was sucked in.

"Hi, Kim. I just wanted to thank you. You're going to be such a help to me, having spent so much time at camp. You can see it from the campers' viewpoint. I really want the kids to have a great experience, but I'll be so focused on keeping them safe, making up their schedules, and enforcing the rules that I might actually lose sight of what's fun for them."

"You must be telepathic. I was just wondering if I made the right decision. To be honest, I don't want to leave you in a bind, but I'm having my doubts now." And I'm way too vulnerable to be around you right now.

"Please, Kim. Give it a chance. If you get there and it's totally wrong for you, you don't have to stay. I'll find someone else, but as long as we're really being honest, it goes beyond camp for me. I was looking forward to getting to know you again."

Why does he have to sound so sincere?

He goes on. "I was wondering if you would consider coming in early on Saturday? Most of the staff will be arriving for our meeting at five. I thought if you came in sooner, I could run the staff agenda by you. Get your feedback. See if I've missed anything important."

Before I can answer, he rushes on. "There's also that little perk of first choice of cabins. Early bird gets the best something. . . and all that."

He's making it so easy to say yes. Like the other night, I find myself falling in step with his plans. "You missed your calling by teaching. You should be in sales." I relent. "I can probably be there by one on Saturday."

"Great! The kitchen doesn't open until Sunday night, but I'll pick up some sandwiches for us."

"By the way, aren't all the instructor cabins the same?" I

ask.

"Yes, but you know, location, location, location. You probably want to be closest to the kitchen. Or laundry. Your choice."

His enthusiasm sounds so genuine that I make a list of what I need to do to leave my condo for ten weeks. I hope it's not a summer I regret.

June 2010
Back to the Future

As soon as I turn off the main highway to the two-lane wooded road leading to the camp, a rush of feelings comes over me. Nothing has changed. I'm ten years old again, bouncing in the back seat of Dad's '85 blue Ford Tempo and screaming, "We're here. We're here."

Now I expected to see new homes. Maybe a whole subdivision, but the woods are still thick. I roll down the windows and breathe in the scent of the trees on each side of the road. I hear the trickle of the stream where I first paddled a canoe.

When I approach the camp entrance, it's like a step back in time. Everything is the same. Two large stone pillars at either end of the wide entry with room for cars to enter and exit at the same time, one stone pillar dividing them. The wooden gate that has to be raised and slid to one side to enter. It normally has a big padlock on it to keep strangers out as well as eager parents on Sunday mornings. I remember as a young camper sitting in a line of cars with my parents, so eager to get in that I asked them every five minutes, "Is it noon yet?"

My father's answer was always the same. "If it was noon, we wouldn't be sitting here, would we?"

As soon as we saw Herb, the caretaker, walking toward the padlock in his slow amble, jingling a huge ring of keys, the car horns started beeping with excitement. He dragged out his five minutes of glory, fumbling with the keys as if he couldn't find the right one while the horns continued to beep. For that brief moment, he was the most important person at Good Acres—the keeper of the gate. The gate that opened a week of fun and adventures.

There's no lock on the gate now, so I get out of my car, swing it wide and drive through. I see that the totem pole is still the first sign of Indian lore that sets the theme for the camp. In vivid colors of red, turquois, and orange, it's as welcoming and bright as ever, just not as tall as I remembered it.

Before I take the winding road to the Lodge, I also recall that the last time I was here as a counselor Mike and I were a couple. My world was full of wonderful possibilities with college ahead and someone who loved me. It was a time when I trusted that life was good. I want so much to have that feeling again. Trusting people, trusting myself. Maybe I'm putting too many expectations on a summer camp to restore my confidence, but perhaps this is a step in the right direction. I can only hope.

I weave the car to the right to begin the climb to the Lodge. The crunch of my tires meeting the gravel road is even a familiar sound.

Herb's stone house sits just within the entrance at the first curve. It's set back under large trees. From the wrap-around porch, he can see any cars coming or leaving camp.

On the final curve, the Lodge comes into view. Four stories high, it's the heart of camp. As I approach it, I see the large concrete area with the flagpole. Each morning we gathered there for revelry, flag raising, The Pledge of Allegiance and exercises. I can see the kids, still drowsy, doing their jumping jacks in a circle. Sleepy jacks we called them. In the evening we lowered the flag to the sound of taps over the loudspeaker once the campers were safe in their bunks.

Pottawatami Cabin. Good Acres. Summer 1987
Dear Diary,

I should have known something was up when everyone went to bed so early and no one was talking. Then I felt something touch my toe. Something slithery—something alive. I screamed and jumped out of bed. When I tore back the blanket, I saw it lying there at the foot of my bed. A green snake. Its tongue flicked back and forth. I couldn't stop screaming even though I suspected it was a harmless garter. First I screamed because I was afraid, but then I kept screaming because I was so mad.

Where was Robin, the counselor? Why did she let this happen?

Someone said, "Wendy, I told you we shouldn't have done it. We're going to be in trouble when Robin gets back."

Then I heard some muffled giggles, stifled by pillows.

I wished I had the courage to grab the snake and put it in Wendy's face. See how much of a nature girl she really is. But I couldn't bring myself to touch it. Let them figure out how to get it out of the cabin. Hopefully it would slither over to Wendy's bed.

I didn't say a word. I just grabbed my pillow and blanket and walked out the door, then headed up the hill to the Lodge where I could sleep on the floor by the big fireplace. As I trudged up the hill, I met my counselor Robin coming down. When she asked me where I was going, I knew if I told what happened the girls would do something worse. I spied the nurse's cabin and said I had a stomachache. Robin walked me to the infirmary.

The nurse was so nice to me. Asked if I wanted to spend the night there. She even gave me a Popsicle. It took me a long time to fall asleep because I kept thinking of ways to get even with Wendy. Nothing came to mind, but I knew someday it would.

Greetings

I pull into the parking area behind the Lodge, and before I can even open my door, Paul comes out of the director's cabin just to the right of the parking spot, waving and smiling.

"My first camper arrives." He runs to open my door. "Can I help you unload?"

Before I can answer, he says, "You need to pick your cabin. Or maybe you'd rather have lunch first. Are you hungry?"

I'm a bit overwhelmed by his greeting. "If you greet each camper this way, you'll get a five-star rating. I just want to stretch my legs a bit. It's a ninety-minute ride from north Chicago."

"Of course. Come on, I'll give you a little tour. Or maybe you should be giving me the tour."

"Seems nothing much has changed. That's for sure. Talk about a time warp."

"Is that good or bad?" He looks concerned.

"It's great." I smile at him and continue, "Okay, let's check out my options here for the next ten weeks." I pivot toward a row of cabins. "First choice?"

"Yeah, first choice of those three." He points to three cabins. "The cooks will share one. Lucy and Courtney asked to be roommates and that leaves Mari, the swim instructor and you. You'll like her. She's our age. The other ones have bunks for the guy instructors and the maintenance boys."

I poke my head in the cabins, but they all look about the same to me. I choose the one on the very end which has a view of trees. It's also directly behind Mike's cabin although farthest from the Lodge and laundry.

"Good choice. I'll carry your luggage in, and then we'll have some lunch."

"I can get unpacked later. Really. Let's go up to the Lodge." In truth, I don't want him to see how much stuff I brought. My car is packed as if I were leaving for my freshman year at college. I head to the door. "Let's go this way. I can't wait to see the front porch again."

We walk to the Lodge, and once on the porch, I spin around to look back down the hill. Just as I remembered. A beautiful clearing of green lawn, sloping down about five hundred feet to the ten rustic log cabins. I can't see the names on them, but I know each one has a plaque over the door with an Indian tribe name, such as Waubansee, Pontiac, Chegagou, Shabbona, and Iroquois, The cabin on the very end, Pottawatami, was where I was both a camper and a counselor. Although everything looks smaller than I remember, virtually nothing has changed.

I have such wonderful memories of Good Acres, but standing here, I have a slight feeling of apprehension. Perhaps it's the stillness? I realize I'd never seen it without one hundred kids running up or down the hill. Surely this summer would be another good memory.

Memories

Lost in my memories while standing on the porch, Paul's voice startles me.

"Sixty-three acres of rolling woodland along the Little Calumet River."

"Really?" I ask. "And where did you get that bit of information?"

"Google, of course. Found some great articles with the entire history of the camp. Surely a good researcher like you did the same."

I laugh. "Actually, I did a little myself yesterday. Did you read the article about the swimming pool?"

We glance just to the right of us in front of the director's cabin, the pool's blue water shimmering crystal clear, inviting the campers' first splashes.

"Something about the first of its kind?" he asks.

"Evidently the camp was designed by U.S. Steel engineers from the huge plant here on Lake Michigan. Its layout was quite modern for its time in 1941. Construction was held up until after the war and finished in 1946. The stainless steel swimming pool brought visitors from as far as Japan, admiring the merits of steel construction."

"See, what did I tell you? There's your first story. Historic Camp Built to Last. Site Still Thrives."

"Speaking of thriving, where's this lunch you promised? I'm starving."

"Me too. I made a run to the old neighborhood last night to see if my favorite Italian restaurant is still in business. Same family, run by the kids now. The neighborhood is looking a little shabby. Dangerous is more like it, but their Italian beef sandwiches are worth the risk."

He leads me into the kitchen and pulls two packages wrapped in white butcher paper out of the fridge. "Can we nuke these?" he asks. "There should be some paper plates in that cupboard there."

When he unwraps them, I laugh. "My gosh, Paul, this is enough for six people. Do you want to split one?"

"No chance," he says. You can cut yours in half if you want. Someone will snarf it up later. I forgot the soft drinks in my cabin fridge. I'll be right back."

When he leaves, I step into the dining room and once again get lost in memories. Long polished, knotty cedar dining tables with picnic-bench seating on each side. Captain's chairs at the head and foot of each table. The massive stone fireplace at one end with a stage in front where we did our talent shows, our skits, movies on rainy days and sing-a-longs. A piano and juke box are in the corner. I'll have to check out what era the 45's are. Probably the originals.

The open balcony with more polished knotty cedar creates a rustic feel, yet the windows make the room bright and sunny.

The ding on the microwave brings me back to present day and I put the beef sandwiches on paper plates. I cut both in half, wondering how I'm going to pick it up, the bread dripping with juice. Paul returns carrying two cans of soda.

"Are you a Pepsi or Coke person?"

"Pepsi for me."

"First choice for you. You realize I'm being nice. Don't

want you running off."

"No chance of that. I forgot how beautiful this place is. Inside and out. Like we're a million miles from everything even though the main highway is just a few miles away. But I did see a new mall on the way in. Civilization encroaches."

One bite into the juicy Italian beef, and I know I'm a goner. Before I know it, I've devoured my whole sandwich.

Paul looks at my plate and laughs. "Are you the one who wanted to share?"

"Well, since you risked your life in the Mafia neighborhood to get these, the least I can do is appreciate it. Evidently, the great outdoors is already working on my appetite."

"Let's unload your car and I'll get my notes for the meeting."

I was trying to avoid that scene, but he's too quick. Eyeing my back seat and trunk he says, "Looks like you've decided to stay the ten weeks." A short laugh. "Or maybe ten years?"

"Very funny. A girl never knows what she might need. If you can get those boxes, I'll take the hanging clothes. I don't remember an ironing board here, so I brought one just in case." I pull out a portable board.

"What in the world would you be ironing?" he asks.

It does seem like a stupid idea now that I remember we'd be wearing the standard camp shorts and tees each day. "Beats me. I never iron at home, but for some reason, I thought I'd better have one. Should I just put this in the laundry room for everyone to use?"

"Yeah, we can pretend it was already here. One of those antiques left over from the beginning of time. I promise I won't tell anyone you brought it, June."

"June?"

"Yeah, June Cleaver."

"Funny. You might as well take the iron with it. You'll probably be the first one begging me to press your Sunday shirt to wow the parents."

"Oh yeah, shirts. I need to show you around the camp store for tomorrow's sale."

We unload the car and leave my boxes in one corner of the cabin. I claim the bed closest to the window by throwing my laptop case and a duffle bag on it. "I'll unpack this stuff later."

Paul takes me into the room set up as the camp store, a sunny room off the main dining room with windows from floor to ceiling. Six-foot tables are spread around the room in a square, covered with tee shirts, nightgowns, sweatshirts and caps. All with the Good Acres logo. Boxes with more clothes under each table. A little cashier station is set up at the doorway.

"Open Sundays one to five, Wednesday nights and Saturdays nine to noon. Tonight the staff gets three tee-shirts free, but they can buy whatever else they want at a discount. There's a hundred dollars in the cash box. Let me know if you need more change. We're not set up for credit cards, but we can take checks. Make sure there's a phone number on them. You can return the cash box to my safe in the cabin."

"Oh, so that's where the big bucks stay?"

"Yep. Fort Knox. I'll make a bank deposit every Monday. Proceeds from the store and canteen."

We head downstairs to the basement. A small one-lane bowling alley, two ping-pong tables, Foosball and a pinball machine. Shelves with games of checkers, chess, Scrabble, and Monopoly.

The canteen is already stocked to the brim with candy bars, ropes of licorice, bags of chips and a freezer full of Popsicles and ice cream bars.

I reach for a candy necklace which I haven't seen in

years. "I've got to have one of these right now."

"Allow me." He takes one off the rack and places it around my neck. "No charge. That's for coming in early."

I have the urge to pop one of the little candies in his mouth which is dangerously close. There's hardly room for two people behind the counter. "When did you get all this stuff in?"

"Oh, I've been here a week. Most of the food deliveries came yesterday. Canteen hours are 3-4 each day and evenings from 6-8."

"Who's doing that?"

"The maintenance team. They'll trade off afternoons and evenings. Most of their day work is done by two."

"You're going to trust those growing hungry boys with all this candy? Hope by the end of the summer you're not too deep in the red."

"Really? Should I have someone else do it? That's why I need your input."

"Just kidding. I'm sure they'll be fine. Tell them you balance the drawer each day."

We walk upstairs and sit at one of the table benches, side by side.

Paul opens a manila folder and places the agenda between us. "I should have made you a copy."

"No problem. We can share," I say. No problem at all except it's hard to concentrate with him so close. He smells so clean, like a fresh bar of soap.

He goes over the agenda point by point and it seems adequate. It seems he wants reassurance more than actual input, and I realize how important it is for him to give the kids a great camp experience. A genuinely nice guy.

Wonder why no one has latched on to him yet? I don't suppose this is the time to bring it up, but it's hard to believe he's still single with no baggage. Maybe there's baggage I don't know about yet. "Well, I should get unpacked."

"Yeah, you might want to get rid of those boxes so your roommate can at least get in the door." He grins.

We head out the front porch. It's one of those rare summer days in the Midwest that isn't dripping with humidity. Probably in the 80's, sunny, with a gentle breeze and big white puffy clouds. I have a strong urge to explore the grounds. "Have you found the path yet?" I ask.

"What path?"

"The sacred path leading to the Friday night bonfire and closing ceremony. The best night of camp."

"Well, if this is my private orientation from a seasoned camper, you'd better show me. Lead the way."

We head down the hill, past the cabins, through the baseball diamond, and further into a clearing behind it.

Just as the woods begin, I see the opening. It would be easy to miss if one wasn't here before. "Follow me. You have to go single file. Only a flashlight to light your way at night. That's the fun of it. No talking. Just like the Indian warriors who walked this ground for hundreds of years in their moccasins. Minus flashlights, of course."

"Google didn't tell me anything about this path."

"It's part of the old Good Acres legend. Spirit of cooperation between the natives and the white man. At the end of the path, campers circle the Bailey Marriage tree, an intertwined oak and elm. It supposedly commemorates the marriage of an early settler to an Indian maiden."

We walk quietly through the woods with sun dappling through the tall tree branches until the path reaches a large clearing.

"Oh my gosh, it's still there." I point across the clearing where the twisted oak and elm tree grew together.

"Wow, this is cool." Paul stands in the clearing with the trees creating a perfect circle.

More memories flood back and I circle the area, gazing upward.

"What are you looking for?"

"The wire. I don't see it. Maybe they stopped using it."

"Okay, translation please."

"When I was a counselor, two of the maintenance boys would soak a roll of toilet paper in kerosene and also douse the logs on the bonfire. They'd climb the tree with the paper roll before the campers arrived. No one could see them up there through the leaves. Then when everyone was seated around the campfire in the dark, the leader—that would be you," I say, pointing to his chest. "—would call the fire gods to light the fire. The boys hidden in the tree would light the toilet roll and send it flying down the wire straight to the bonfire which lit up the minute it hit. A flame of fire straight from the fire gods in the sky. I must say it was pretty dramatic."

Paul peers up at the trees, "I like it. Let's see if we can bring it back without burning down the entire woods. Good thing it's been a rainy season."

We sit down on one of the long logs forming a square around the campfire site. I can't resist nibbling on my candy necklace.

"I wonder how old that thing is." Paul studies the intertwined oak and elm marriage tree.

"It's lasted longer than most marriages, I can tell you that." As soon as I say it, I regret sounding like a whiner. "What about you?" I ask. "I keep wondering why someone as nice as you isn't married. If you don't mind my asking."

"I don't mind. Once I got really close. I met her about four years ago. She taught at my school. Came from Alabama. A real southern belle. We dated about a year and a half. Got engaged at Christmas and the wedding was to be the following June."

"What happened?"

"She went back home to visit her grandmother who was dying. It was spring break. When she came back, she called off the wedding. Said she was moving back to Alabama as soon as the school year was over. Said she never should have left the south. It was home. She left that May and I never heard from her again. Another teacher told me that she married one of the 'good ole boys' from home. It never made sense to me, but I'm over it now. That was about two years ago."

"Maybe Grandma was going to cut her out of the will if she married a Yankee."

He laughs. "You probably speak the truth."

"So, has there been anyone else since then?"

"Not really. A few dates here and there, usually arranged by well-meaning friends. It never seems to pan out. That's another reason I took this job. Thought it would be nice to have a big family to come home to each night."

"Come home to? They'll be in your home night and day. Are you sure you're ready for this?"

"No, I'm not sure of anything. Wait, I take that back. I'm sure glad you're here." He stands and reaches down to pull me up with both hands.

"I'm glad too." With a smile, I brush the dust off my shorts. "Just follow me."

"Anywhere," he says.

Meet and Greet

The staff trickles in all afternoon Saturday for the meeting scheduled at five. Pizzas are being delivered at seven. Those returning greet one another with hugs and grins.

Several familiar refrains seep through my open door and window as I unpack. Here we go again. How you been? Great to see you.

My roommate, Mari, the swim coach, arrives with a boatload of stuff, which makes me feel better. I know we're going to get along great when she carries in a fan and a small coffeepot.

She says, "Hi, I'm Maribelle, but everyone calls me Mari. I can't function without a cup of coffee first thing, but I'm not walking to the Lodge in my pjs for it."

Mari has the sleek body of someone who has spent hours in the water and straight short blond hair that will probably bleach even lighter by the end of the summer in the pool. A junior high phys-ed teacher, Mari grew up near here, but has never been to Good Acres. She did teach swimming at a camp in the Upper Peninsula of Michigan.

I help her unpack her car and we talk as we make trips from car to cabin.

She says, "We moved to Michigan for my husband's job.

He travels so much I never see him except on weekends anyway, so this was a perfect summer job for me. And a chance to spend time with my parents."

Besides our two beds, the only furniture in the room are one high dresser and a short one. She suggests I take the short one as a makeshift desk to set my computer on. Conveniently one of the few outlets in the room is right behind it. I'll find a folding chair in the Lodge. That's pretty much it. Shower, sink and toilet are in the only other room. To call it a room is a stretch. More like a closet.

Mari says, "Maybe I'll pick up some cheap lawn chairs this weekend for us. We can keep them outside our front door. We scored the best cabin. A little shade here on the corner and closest to the pool."

"That was my incentive for coming early," I say. I don't add the part about having four hours alone with Paul, hoping my feelings won't become too transparent to the staff. Feelings I'm not even sure about myself. I keep reminding myself this is about a fun summer. Not about a romance. I'm not ready for romance.

By five o'clock everyone is sitting at the picnic benches in the main dining room—the heart of camp.

Paul seems comfortable in front of the group. "Okay, I'll start with the positives. As you know, this will be the only Saturday night you are required to stay at the campgrounds. For the next ten weeks—five weeks for girl counselors—you'll be off from noon on Saturday until eleven on Sunday. You're welcome to stay on the grounds as long as you know that there are no meals furnished. Cooks need a night off too."

He nods toward two older women sitting together, both with white hair. "But if you're nice, they might show you where they keep the leftovers." Snickers all around.

Edna and Mabel beam. They're both a bit plump, which

makes me happy. I could never trust a skinny cook.

"And as you know, this is my first summer here, so I welcome any suggestions and input from those of you who have been here before. I'm committed to keeping things the way they've always been, so if I'm not doing something that was special to you from years past, just let me know. Most of the fun things are not in the policy and procedures book they gave me."

Some laughter and someone says, "That's for sure."

I sense the acceptance of him from the group with that simple acknowledgement that he doesn't have all the answers. I'm liking him a little more with every situation.

Then he holds up two decks of cards with different designs on the back. He divides us into two groups and has us each pick a card from either deck. "Find the matching card and you've got your partner for our first icebreaker."

There's an even number of us, including Paul, for a total of twenty-six. The staff consists of director, Paul; two cooks, Edna and Mabel; the nurse, JoAnna; two lifeguards, Jesse and Brett; Swimming, Mari; Kevin, PE and riflery; Courtney, drama and music; Lucy, archery; and myself for arts and crafts. There's also ten cabin counselors, mostly college age; four maintenance boys, high school freshmen, who love getting behind the wheels of the tractors since they don't have their real driver's licenses yet, and Herb the caretaker, age unknown, but rumored to be as old as the Lodge itself, now sixty-nine years old.

Paul puts a list of questions on a flip chart to ask our partners. The usual: Where are you from? Have you been to camp before? Why do you want to work here?

I draw the queen of spades and see a young girl with a long ponytail, her hair as black as the queen of spades she is waving.

She runs to me. "Hi. My name's Jordan and I'm so glad

to be here. I've wanted to be a counselor ever since I was a camper."

If she were a dog, she'd have licked my face. The campers and parents will love her because her enthusiasm is infectious. I find myself wishing I could be in her cabin. Only for about two minutes when I picture the washhouse.

At one point, Paul's laugh reaches my ears and I see that he's paired with Lucy, the archery instructor. He's leaning back against one of the picnic tables and she's standing so close they're almost eye to eye. Any closer and they'd be touching. Whatever made him laugh now seems to have him spellbound as his eyes focus on her the whole time she's talking.

A wave of jealousy comes over me. What is wrong with me? He is not my partner in this exercise—or in life. It's just the insecurity I've felt ever since I caught Mike with BB. I hate this feeling.

I turn to Jordan and ask her something that will divert my attention.

Then Paul calls us back together. "Can someone share something interesting about their partner?"

Lucy quickly raises her hand.

"My partner was Paul," and she grins as if she's found the prize in the Cracker Jack box.

"What's interesting about Paul is that he's not married."

Everyone laughs. Paul blushes. I cringe.

Mari, the swim coach, says, "My partner was JoAnna, the nurse. During the year she works in the public schools. She says the campers are her main focus, but she's here for us too. But she doesn't have any medication for hangovers."

More laughs. Paul joins in, "That's good and it reminds me. You probably all know the rule, 'No liquor on the grounds or it's grounds for dismissal.' I hope you all make it through the summer."

Jordan raises her hand and I feel a moment of apprehension. I became so engrossed with Paul and Lucy, I can't remember what I told her.

"My partner was Kim and this is her eighth summer at Good Acres."

That seems to impress some, and others look at me as though I'm some sort of sicko kid who never grew up.

Paul smiles at me and says, "If we give out lifetime achievement awards, Kim would qualify."

"Oh no, that goes to Herb," Edna, the cook, pipes in. "He's been here thirty-five, or is it thirty-six years?"

Herb beams, obviously pleased of the recognition. "This is my thirty-sixth year."

Everyone claps and one would have thought he was getting the Purple Heart. Probably deserves it. He does look like a WWII vet with his silver hair cropped to a crew cut of the fifties.

I want to reward Jordan for her enthusiasm so I raise my hand. "My partner, Jordan, is a counselor for the first time. With her enthusiasm I know her cabin kids are going to have a great summer."

Paul says, "Great. That leads us to our next question and activity. When campers go home, what do you want them to tell their parents and friends about their experience here?"

A few hands go up and the answers are what one would expect. "It was the best week of my life. I made new friends."

Mari says, "I want them to say, 'I learned not to be afraid of the deep end."

Edna, with a hairdo that reminds me of Aunt Bee in Mayberry, says, "This is what I hope they don't say. 'The food was really yukky.'"

We all agree that we don't want them to say that, as most of us will also have ten weeks of the same food.

JoAnna, the nurse, says, "I hope no one goes home

saying the other kids were mean to them."

The exercise serves its purpose, as we all relax a bit and realize that although we come from many backgrounds, we have a lot in common. Many are teachers—who else could take the summer off— and people who like kids and the outdoors. No one is expecting a five-star hotel experience. Although we aren't roughing it in the true sense of the word, the cabins are rustic, the mosquitoes can be fierce, and the schedule can get tedious doing the same thing week after week.

Paul has written all the answers on a flip chart. Since they reflect a positive experience for the kids, he then asks us each to think of what special quality we have—one we plan to put to use daily—that would make this a reality for the kids. After pizza, we'll talk about our personal commitment to the campers.

The last question makes me realize if I were a parent, I'd want someone like him to be running this camp. It also makes me realize he'd make a great parent. I can't be thinking this way. It's too soon.

A trickle of shame circulates when I realize that most of my motivation in coming here was self-centered. To have a change of scenery, and if totally honest, to get to know Paul. It seems I've been thinking mostly of the benefits to myself and not the campers. True, I had short notice and was pitching in at the last minute, but now I need to focus on the kids. This is not my therapy camp—it's their time to grow and to have fun. Get my mindset in perspective here.

While we're eating, Paul calls our attention to a table at the back of the room with scrapbooks and photo albums on it. "Someone's been pretty good about recording the history of Good Acres. If you'd like to see pictures of the staff— since the beginning of time, have at it."

One of the maintenance boys interrupts, ""'erb, is your

baby picture there?"

Herb laughs along with the others. The maintenance boys are his responsibility and obviously they have already bonded. When Herb laughs, I think of Santa Claus. And his belly shook when he laughed, like a bowl full of jelly. It also reminds me that we often celebrated Christmas in July at camp. I need to tell Paul about the decorations we used to keep in the storage closet.

"Getting back to the albums," Paul is saying. "We have a photographer coming tonight. Thought we'd get a staff picture while you're fresh and excited."

Someone says, "Maybe we should do a before-and-after the ten weeks. See if we can even recognize ourselves."

Someone else remarks, "Yep, fresh and excited might look more like tired and battered."

It's a tribute to Paul that the staff is commenting freely.

While others are finishing their pizza, I go to the back table and thumb through the albums. I do the math—ten years old my first year. That would have been about 1987. I find a photo of our cabin, Pottawatami, same as the photo in my scrapbook at home. The grins and goofy faces bring back memories. I doubt I'd recognize anyone if I met them today.

Then I see the photo of my last year, 1995—a group shot of just the cabin counselors. Ten of us. I haven't spoken to any of these girls since that time. We promised to stay in touch, but most of us were off to our first year of college. I would have been eighteen that last summer.

Wouldn't it be fun to see where everyone was now? We could meet here on a Saturday night—maybe have a cookout. They could bring their families if they wanted to. I'd have to run the idea past Paul. I slip the photo out of its plastic seal to show him what I have in mind.

"I don't think you're supposed to remove those," a voice behind me says. I turn to see JoAnna. "It's probably the only photo they have—the history of camp."

"Oh, I won't keep it. I just want to show it to Paul and ask him about a possible reunion of this group. Wouldn't that be fun?"

"What a great idea. What year would that be?"

I show her the photo. She studies intently as if she's looking for someone.

"Are you in any of these old photos?" I ask.

"I've only been the nurse two years, so you probably won't find me in the archives."

The photographer shows up right on schedule. He arranges us in front of the huge stone fireplace where most of the staff photos had been posed, a few of us standing on benches behind the first row, some sitting cross-legged in front. He says he'll take several shots to make sure everyone looks good.

The man's a real comedian as he tries to find different ways to make us smile for each shot. "It's mail call. From your sweetheart. They miss you. Your mom sent cookies. Now smile one last time. Some of you have been here before. Think of your best day ever at camp and how much fun it was." When he's having trouble pulling the desired effect, he says, "Come on now, I need smiles from everyone…There, on the end." He points to JoAnna. "No frowning. Remember the fun times."

Pottawatami Cabin. Good Acres. Summer 1987
Dear Diary.

This morning, Sara said, "Oh, it smells like pee in here." When the counselor checked our sheets, she found a big yellow stain on mine. I must have wet the bed when I saw the snake. The counselor made me hang my sheet out to dry on the line where we hang our bathing suits. Now the whole camp knows I wet the bed, thanks to Sara. She might as well have waved it on the flagpole we stand around to say the pledge each morning. I'm making my own pledge— someday I'll let Sara know how it feels to be humiliated.

Team Building

After pictures, we return to the dining room tables. Herb sits with the cooks. As a widower, he is surely looking forward to three square meals a day, although judging by his size, he hasn't missed too many on his own.

When I was at camp, supposedly there was a Mrs. Herb. As kids we never saw her and wondered if she existed. Stories floated around that the elusive Rosemary—that's the "herb" name we gave her—only came out at night. Ghost stories and legends—all part of a great camp experience. Crazy Man Wilson was also rumored to walk the grounds at night, although he was never seen.

In spite of the opening mixers, everyone returns to the seats they had when they first came in. Counselors sit together and the instructors gather at another long wooden table. The picnic benches on each side hold three to four adults comfortably or five to six small kid bottoms. During the week, each cabin sits at the same table with their counselor.

I now remember the first Sunday night activity after games and relays on the front lawn. Each cabin makes a centerpiece for their table as one of their first team-building activities. As the arts-and-crafts person, I'll suggest it to Paul for Sunday night and see if I have the supplies for it.

I can vividly picture the hideous centerpiece my cabin

made one year. We all loved E.T and tried to replicate the scene where he's in the bike basket flying across the moon. It was a bit too ambitious a project, but it served its purpose of team building. We laughed about what a disaster it was at every meal, and our mantra became, "E.T. Call Home."

Paul is wrapping it up. "We're going to be a family for ten weeks. The campers will come and go. Our time with the campers is really short, but our family time—that's us, the staff—we're here for the long haul. We have to remember that the campers and parents who arrive each Sunday are expecting a staff full of energy. The last group in the summer deserves as much attention and enthusiasm as the first group. Perhaps this talk isn't important tonight when you're all excited. Maybe I should save it for the last week of camp, huh?"

Then Kevin, the P.E. guy, reminds Paul that the last group is made up of twelve-year old boys—often the most challenging. Kevin says, "Camp should start with the oldest kids while we're fresh and end with the seven-year-olds. Those are the easiest. Except maybe their homesickness."

Paul then talks about homesick kids and how we can help them.

Kevin adds, "Anyone remember the director who had a waterbed? He'd let the homesick kids sleep on it in the afternoon. Then they made a big deal out of telling the other campers they got to sleep on the waterbed."

"Did that help?" Paul asks.

"It might have helped the camper, but I heard later that the director got a divorce."

Everyone laughs.

"I suppose it would test a marriage to have homesick campers in your bed for ten weeks," Paul says.

Lucy snickers and whispers to Courtney, "If I get homesick, would Paul let me recover on his bed?"

I hear her but Paul doesn't. He's moved on to bullies. "Any signs you see of kids being excluded, let others on the staff know. Let's all be prank or bully detectives."

Mari, the swim coach, says, "You know I hate to see a child picked on, but sometimes those kids bring it on themselves. I remember a kid when I went to camp. It wasn't here, but at a camp we spent four weeks at, so everyone's real personality came out. There was a girl in our cabin who got a cookie-care package every week, large enough to feed the entire camp. I'm sure her mother meant for her to share it. She probably already suspected the girl would have trouble making friends. But Kendra—that was her name—never shared. Of course, her cabin mates resented her, not to mention the bugs her stash attracted."

JoAnna is nodding her head. "I see children with stomachaches and headaches, but many times it's heartache, disguised as other ailments that brings them to my cabin. You can only do so much with a Tylenol."

"Good point, JoAnna." Paul responds.

"Let's come up with some specific suggestions. How can we help those children—those who are excluded and those who do the excluding?"

"Call the parents. Tell them pickup time has been changed to Wednesday," Billy says.

More laughs.

Courtney says, loud enough for our table to hear but not Paul, as his back is turned and he's writing on the flip chart. "You can list suggestions 'til that marker runs dry, but kids will be kids. Nothing changes. It happened when I was a camper, and it will keep on as long as kids this age are forced to live together."

I find myself wanting to protect Paul. He doesn't need the jaded opinions or apathy of the seasoned staffer. His concern is genuine, but it seems some of the veterans are humoring him. I scan the counselor table. They seem to be listening intently, and perhaps that's the most important group for that message, as they spend more time with the campers than the instructors.

Paul then reminds us that the campers are also watching us. "If they see any disputes among us, we're not setting a good example for harmony at camp. You've probably heard this since most of you have been here before, but the founders wanted campers to learn sportsmanship, democratic living, proper etiquette, outdoor appreciation and spirituality during their week."

"So no food fights?" one of the counselors asks.

"Well, not in front of the kids," Paul is quick to reply.

I can tell he is earning the respect of the staff with his easy manner and quick wit. He's also scoring a few points with me.

He goes on. "In closing, I expect you to play well with others—your fellow staff members."

"I wouldn't mind playing nice with him," Lucy whispers to Courtney.

"Well, you're the archery lady. Why don't you just play Cupid with that bow and arrow of yours?" Courtney laughs at her own play on words.

I glance at Lucy. She's cute in an all-American-girl way. Short blond hair in a stylish cut, not much makeup and big brown eyes. In her intro, Paul said she had been teaching third grade for five years—that would make her younger than I am if she began teaching right out of college. It seems everybody is younger these days. She's wearing khaki short shorts that show off nice legs and a low-cut white tee showing cleavage that doesn't look like any camp shirt I remember. Isn't there a dress code here?

I look down at the baggy Good Acres sweatshirt I bought myself to wear when the kids arrive, thinking I might sell more if I modeled the goods. Obviously, Lucy is selling something too, but it isn't to the campers.

My insecurities since Mike's affaire are surfacing again. To my surprise, hot tears form. I blink my eyes to keep them from spilling over. Maybe I'm not emotionally stable enough to take on this job yet. How am I going to help some homesick, insecure kid when I'm starting all over myself, and one simple word or action brings on tears? I feel as insecure as a little kid myself, leaving her mom on the first day of school. Except now I have no hand or dress hem to cling to.

I bolt before anyone at the table sees me and head to one of the kitchen sinks to splash cold water on my now burning cheeks. When I return to the main dining room, I wave to Paul and point to the store to remind him it's time for staff shopping.

He says, "Hey, everybody. If you want to buy more shirts, the store will be open for about thirty minutes tonight. Ten percent discount for staff."

Some of the counselors head for the front porch, the two cooks announce that Sunday night dinner will be the traditional sloppy joes and mac and cheese—the ultimate comfort foods.

As I pass Herb, I hear him ask Edna when she's going to reveal the secret ingredient in her sloppy joe recipe.

"Probably never, Herb. Then it wouldn't be a secret, would it?"

"I'm good at keeping secrets," he says with a twinkle in his eye.

I alerted Paul about the summer romances that usually play out on the third floor between staff and counselors. Perhaps a little romance going on in the kitchen too? I smile at the thought of it.

Lucy is wiggling her way to Paul, who's tearing the

sheets off the flip chart to post in the staff lounge on the second floor. He told me he was going to tape them right above the computer with Internet access so we could be constantly reminded of our commitment. Good plan, although I doubt flip charts can compete with surfing the net. But worth a try, perhaps like subliminal popcorn commercials at the movies.

Lucy says something that causes Paul to smile, but as I walk past them to head to the store, I hear him say that he still has some things to do in his office for tomorrow's registration

Paul calls my name. "Kim, can I see you after you close the store? A few minutes."

"Sure," No, I'm sneaking out the gate for a hot late date. My sarcasm often surfaces when I'm hurt or angry.

He catches up and says, "I need to ask you a few things."

"And I just remembered a fun project I had forgotten until tonight. One is for tomorrow night," I add.

The thumbs-up he gives me tells me that maybe an oversized sweatshirt is the thing to wear after all.

Finding My Counselors

Sunday morning, sitting at a table in the dining room, I study the counselor group photo I took from the album. I had put it in a manila folder like I do when I begin to gather information for my free-lance assignments. On the tab I write, Counselor Reunion.

I take a clean sheet of lined paper and make a list of names. Wonder how many I'll actually find with just their maiden names to go by. Like myself, many of them have probably moved out of the area, but perhaps their parents are still here. Of the nine high schools in the surrounding area, it's strange that I'm the only one from my school in the picture or I might have touched base with someone at the class reunion.

My list reads as follows:
Wendy Mickovich
Nancy Morris
Barb Bailey
Diane Minick
Sara Scordoto
Laurie Mayer
Kathy Knoles
Lois Betka

Should I make phone calls or Google? If they've

married, Google probably wouldn't be much help. I go with the calls. I remember the old pay phone booth in the basement of the Lodge and sure enough there's a battered book hanging from a chain. The date on the cover says 1989. It's seen better days. I'm hoping it's not too early on a Sunday morning to be making calls and I'll possibly miss those who go to church. If they have answering machines, I can leave my cell number.

Cell phones and the Internet connection are the only things about camp that have changed. Years ago, we had to use the pay phone in the basement. In an emergency, we could use the phone in the director's office or the nurse's cabin.

I find two Mickovich's in the phone book. No Wendy, just a John and Pete.

After two rings of the John number, I hear a frail, "Hello."

"Mrs. Mickovich?"

"Yes." She sounds reluctant as if I'm a telemarketer.

"I'm trying to locate Wendy. Is this the right Mickovich?"

"Why do you want to know?" Her voice takes on a sharp tone.

"My name is Kim Douglas. I went to Good Acres with Wendy many years ago. I'm working at the camp again this summer and thought it would be nice to have a reunion of the counselors. Is Wendy still in the area?"

There's no answer so I ask, "Mrs. Mickovich, are you there?"

"I'm here all right, but Wendy's not. She's buried at Memorial Gardens."

"Oh my gosh, I'm so sorry. I had no idea. Please forgive me for calling."

Her voice sounds sympathetic to me now. "I'm sure you didn't know. It's just so hard. Especially when the anniversary rolls around. It was such a shock."

"Do you mind my asking, was she ill?"

"No, it was a tragic accident. A snakebite of all things. A freak accident. I'm not up to talking about this now. Good luck with your plans."

With a click, she disconnects.

That takes me back a step and I pause, not sure I want to make another call. But I can't stop on a negative note.

I make the second call. Nancy.

A man answers, and for a moment I hesitate, still a little disturbed by the first call.

"Mr. Morris?"

"Yes," he answers in a pleasant voice which makes me feel better.

"Mr. Morris, my name is Kim Douglas and I went to Good Acres with a Nancy Morris many years ago. We were counselors together. I'm trying to locate her now and wonder if you are related to her?"

"Yes, Nancy's my daughter. You young ladies had quite the time at camp, didn't you? Nancy still talks about it from time to time."

I breathe a huge sigh of relief. "I'm working at the camp this summer and thought it would be fun to have a reunion of the counselors. Does Nancy live in the area?"

"No, she's on the west coast, but I bet she'd love to hear from you. Let me get you her number. I have her email too if you'd like."

"Oh, that would be great." I know I'm gushing, so glad to make a connection. I'm also impressed that he seems to be in the twenty-first century with an email account.

I dial the number he gives me and leave a voice message, with a note beside her name to follow up with an email.

The response to his call inspires me to keep going. My third call to Barb has no answer but an answering machine asks me to leave a message, which I do.

Moving down the list to Diane, I dial and am told that no one by that name lives there, nor do they know a Diane. I write Google beside her name.

I scan down the list. Number five. Sara Scordoto. Can't be too many names like that in the phone book. I find one listing. First initial E. I dial and discover that it's her aunt.

I explain the purpose of my call and am told that Sara's parents retired to Florida. They wanted a fresh start after Sara's death.

Sara dead? Another counselor dead?

"Mrs. Scordoto, I'm so sorry to hear that. Was it an accident, if you don't mind my asking?"

"Worse than an accident. Someone killed her. It was terrible. They found her strangled with a bedsheet. Who could want to hurt Sara? You know she was the sweetest thing. Would never hurt a fly. Her parents were devastated. At least they have Emily and Hannah, Sara's little twins. Her husband's good about having the kids visit their grandparents. This year they're going to spend two weeks in Florida. I just spoke to Sara's mother yesterday and they're taking the little ones to Disney World."

I reply, "How wonderful," with false sincerity, as if Mickey Mouse and Pluto can compensate for a dead mother. I can hardly keep my attention on what she is saying. Two counselors my age dead? How strange is that?

I look at my list. My enthusiasm for this project is fading as fast as the sunshine. The sky has clouded over and thunder rumbles in the distance. I decide to abandon the project, feeling chilled inside and out. Hot coffee. I need coffee. As staff, I'm glad we have kitchen privileges at any time as long as we clean up and don't tap into the actual meal supplies.

Something warm. Something comforting. Most things in the camp kitchen are industrial size, and all I can find is the thirty-cup coffee maker. I could go back to my cabin where Mari, thank goodness, has already brewed a morning pot. But I try the cupboard Paul designated for counselor supplies and find tea bags, fill a mug with water and set the microwave for two minutes. Standing there leaning against the center island, I think again how strange these calls are turning out. A sense of foreboding fills me and somehow my excitement for the reunion has waned. Perhaps it's a stupid idea. I'm not sure I'll even continue with the calls.

I watch the digital numbers on the microwave count down. When I reach in for the cup, the handle is too hot. As I turn to find a towel or potholder, I let out a gasp. Standing less than a foot behind me is JoAnna, dressed in her white nurse's uniform.

She steps back.

"I'm sorry, I didn't mean to startle you." The way she says it, I feel like it's my fault for being startled.

"I didn't hear you," I say.

"I should have said something," she admits.

"No, no, I'm just a little jumpy right now. I've had some disturbing news and I was deep in thought."

"Oh, can I help?"

"No, it's nothing really." Unless you can pop me a little Prozac... might be the thing. My nerves are a little frazzled.

The sky has darkened, and I see a flash of jagged lightning through the windows. From habit, I count and on five, the thunder booms right over our heads.

"Only five miles away. Darn, I hope it stops. I hate to have the campers start off on a rainy, muddy day. Rainy days are bad enough during the week, but that first day of exploring the campgrounds, well, I'd hate for them to miss it. It was always my favorite day, especially when I came back year after year. To make sure things were just the same as I'd left them."

"And were they?"

"Of course, just looking smaller each year. And now after fifteen years, they have really shrunk." I remove the tea bag and take a sip to see if it has cooled off enough to drink. "How about you?" Did you come here as a kid?" I'm racking my brain to try and remember what her partner said about her in the introduction last night.

She hesitates. "No, I didn't. That's why I was glad to get the position. At last, my chance to have fun at camp. A few years late but still not one I wanted to miss."

"Can I fix you a cup of tea? Looks like we might be stuck in the Lodge for a while."

"No. I can beat the rain back to my cabin."

JoAnna walks out and I stand there sipping my tea, trying to decide if I should finish the calls or watch the storm roll in from the safety of the covered front porch.

I walk to the porch and sit in one of knotty cedar chairs just as I see JoAnna run up the stairs of her cabin. Why had she even come up to the Lodge? She must have been in there before I came to the porch. I didn't see her come through the front door. And what's with the uniform? I don't remember our nurse ever wearing one at camp. Maybe she wants to impress the parents with her Sunday best.

Sipping my tea as the downpour begins, I decide that if the storm lets up soon, I will finish the calls. Even if I only reach one or two of the former counselors, it would be great to see them. My cell phone will be crackling with the thunder and lightning all around me, so I wait on the front porch and let the camp memories return.

I gaze at the cabin where I spent my summers. Pottawatami. From the Lodge it's the one on the far left end. The ones in the middle are closest to the washhouse, but we liked being on the end. We always said we were Number One. Later as a counselor, I requested to be in Pottawatami again, out of some kind of loyalty.

I check my watch. About an hour until the gates open. From what I remember, some of the eager parents will be lining up soon, anxious to be the first ones in, and then it will be a steady stream of cars crunching up the winding gravel road to the Lodge for registration. I'll see them as they come through the camp store—kids begging their parents for every conceivable item of clothing that sports the GAC camp logo.

More Calls

The door to the Lodge opens and Paul walks out to the porch wearing navy blue shorts and a blue and white-striped camp tee shirt. The whistle that will become a permanent fixture around his neck is already in place. He looks like a big kid. A very cute big kid.

"Is this a bad omen? A storm my first day of camp?"

"One way to look at it is it can only get better."

"Well, it had better get better," he says. "Are you ready to entertain a hundred campers indoors for the rest of the day?"

"Who says we have to stay indoors? Mud fights are great ice-breakers." I smile and raise my eyebrows as if I've suggested a clandestine affaire. "It might be a good idea to wait for the parents to leave," I warn.

"Now you're really making me nervous. Have I told you lately how glad I am you're here? You've probably spent more time here than the whole staff put together."

"Yeah, yeah, you tell me that every time you see me," I try to blow it off, but each time he says it, it feels good. My wounded psyche needs all the praise it can get. I hate that I feel so needy at times.

He peers at me with those warm brown eyes. "I'm really going to be leaning on you. You don't mind, do you?"

Mind? His firm body leaning on mine? Right now in this storm would be a good time to start. Thunder rumbling. We could be doing some rumbling of our own? Elton John's I Guess That's Why They Call It The Blues plays in my mind.

All this flashes through my mind while I answer. "I'm thinking a raise in pay. That measly wage doesn't exactly cover consulting, especially after hours."

"You know I don't have a dime to spare in this budget. Maybe I could compensate with a Saturday night dinner for two? Isn't there a great steak house a few miles from here?"

"You mean Charley's is still around? Those were the best steaks in the world. Or maybe they just seemed that way after weeks of camp food. Don't tell Edna."

"Hey, speaking of Saturday nights, are you going to call your friends for that reunion you talked about?"

"Actually, that project's not going very well. You'd think it was fifty years ago that we were here instead of fifteen. Two out of five counselors have already died."

"What?"

"Yeah, I thought it was kind of strange myself. You want to hear what's even worse?"

"Oh sure, make my day. Rain, mud-fights, dead counselors. Go ahead—see if you can make it more morbid."

"Seriously, Paul. It is morbid. One was bitten by a snake and the other was strangled with a bedsheet."

"Are you making this up? Sounds like you're getting in practice for camp ghost stories."

"I wouldn't joke about dead people. People I knew."

"Sorry, it's just so bizarre."

"Yeah, tell me about it."

The rain has let up and in the distance I see a patch of blue sky. "Won't be long now till the stampede arrives. You may have a sunny day after all. Do you need me to do anything besides the camp store?"

"No, but I know where to find you if things get crazy. I'm going to check the registration tables one more time."

"Then I'll finish these calls. Only four to go. I'm not going to let my imagination creep me out. I won't have any time the rest of the week once those campers roll in."

Number six on the list is Trish Whipple. I look again at the group picture in the folder. Trish had naturally curly red hair. On a humid day like today, she'd be a real frizz ball out of control, trying to tie it back in a ponytail. Her freckles got darker and closer together as the summer went by. She hated them while I always thought she was the cutest Norman Rockwell girl. My already dark complexion only got darker as the summer went on. When we did the skit with Native Americans, I was always chosen to be the token Navajo princess.

I dialed the first Whipple in the phone book. There were three of them. I hoped that someone would answer and tell me their daughter was healthy and happy.

A kind lady answered both the phone and my wish. "Trish has the most adorable little girl you could imagine," she says.

"Does she have red hair and freckles?"

"No, Betsy looks just like her daddy. Dark hair, straight as string, but she has Trish's big green eyes. She's just a joy to us."

She tells me Trish is in the area. I jot down her number and put a big smiley face next to her name on my list. I get her voice mail and leave a message. The storm has lifted and so have my spirits—I'm glad I continued.

Number seven. Laurie Mayer. I found several Meyers in the book, but not with an a. I write "no phone" beside her name. Maybe Trish can help me since she still lives here.

Number eight. Kathy Knoles. Another unusual spelling of a common name. I find one in the book. There's no answer or voice mail.

The last one on the list is Lois Betka. Two Betkas listed. I call one. No answer. The second call answers Hello on the third ring by someone who sounds like she's out of breath.

"I'm trying to reach Lois Betka. This is an old friend, Kim Douglas, from Good Acres Camp—" I can't even finish before I hear a cheerful response.

"Kim? Kim Douglas? It's me, Lois. What a surprise. After all these years. Oh my gosh, we were just talking about Good Acres the other night. My brother and I. His boys are going there for the first time this summer."

I was so happy to hear her chirpy voice. It made all the other calls worthwhile.

"You aren't going to believe this, but I'm working there this summer."

"Get out. What in the world would you be doing?"

I give her the short version of my long saga.

She replies with, "I'm so jealous. I want to make moccasins again and walk the dark path to the campfire. Can I come visit just once?"

I laugh. "Of course you can, but be careful. This new director will try to recruit you—for measly pay."

"You mean you get paid to have all that fun? Did we get paid? I've forgotten so much. Gosh, I'm dying to talk to you, but I gotta run. We're all late for Sunday school—and I'm the teacher. Can you call me tonight? I really have to go."

A child's voice in the background. "Mom, we're going to be really late."

"Gotta go. I'll call you back."

I have to smile as I hang up the phone. Some people never change. Lois was always late to everything. Her campers kept her on schedule. Wonder why she still has her maiden name? Guess we'll catch up later.

An Ariel View
Opening Day

If on a June Sunday at noon, one were in a small, silent plane or hot air balloon hovering over the campground with the uncanny ability to see through walls, windows and roofs, one might observe the following: Herb shuffling to unlock the gate, cars streaming in slowly and steadily. Ten counselors, each seated at their cabin's picnic bench in the Lodge dining room ready to meet and greet the seven and eight-year-old girls they will spend the next six days with.

Paul at the registration table on the front porch welcoming parents. Nurse JoAnna seated beside Paul to accept and record any medications parents have brought for their children. Instructors milling around, eager and ready to show both the parents and the campers the variety of activities available—swimming, archery, canoeing, crafts. The cooks, Edna and Mabel, in their starched white uniforms offering ice-tea and pastries to the parents and giving them a tour of the massive stainless-steel appliances in the kitchen which will provide the many meals all summer.

If our aerial tour extends to the close of the day after TAPS is played over the loudspeaker, we would see ten campers per cabin, some sitting cross-legged on their cots, some gathered around their counselor's bed for a nighttime story. We would see the instructors on the third-floor lounge listening to music, Mari in her cabin writing a quick letter to her husband in Michigan describing the first splash into the pool, and Paul and Kim on the front porch swing commenting how smoothly the day went.

In the cooks' cabin Mabel in her chenille robe is saying her nightly prayers and choosing a scripture to share with the campers the following morning as they walk through the line where she is filling their plates. She highlights Philippians 4:4.

Of course, she will paraphrase it enough that she can't be accused of preaching religion. As she places hash browns on each plate, she'll simply smile and say, "Rejoice, rejoice. Rejoice in this day the Lord has made."

In the nurse's cabin, JoAnna is bent over her journal. Possibly a list of children's medications?

Emma, the Bookworm

The girls ages seven to nine have been here two days when I first notice her apart from the group. She wears thick lens glasses with cute pink frames and seems smaller than the rest of the girls in her cabin. She's sitting in the shade of an oak tree with her book.

I sit down beside her. "That must be a really good book. You've been reading it for a long time now." I recognize the familiar blue and yellow cover from all the Nancy Drew books I devoured myself as a young girl.

"It's hard to put a good mystery down until you're done." She shows me the cover, The Secret of the Old Clock. "I just have to find out what happens to Allison. If she's going to get the money from the will for her singing lessons. They can't find the last Will and Testament, but I know there is one. Nancy will find it."

"That's the first of the series. It was one my favorites."

"Really? You read Nancy Drew?"

"Well, I used to. Now I read other mysteries. It's nice to know that when you've read all the Nancy Drew books, there will be other good mystery books for you to read."

"When I'm done, I'm going to read them over."

"But won't you know how the mystery is solved when you read them the second time?"

"That's okay. Then I'll read it and recognize the clues as

I go along. There are always lots of clues. Sometimes you miss them the first time. They want you to miss them so you're surprised at the end."

"You're probably right about that."

I notice she's using a torn and ragged piece of paper as a bookmark. "Don't you come to my arts and crafts class in the morning?"

"Yes, I'm making a handprint for my grandpa. He lives in the stone house where we come into camp. He'll like it. He likes everything I make."

"Oh, you must be Emma. This is your first time here, isn't it?" I remember Paul telling me that Herb's granddaughter would be a camper.

"It's my first time as a camper, but I've been to the campgrounds a lot at Grandpa's house. He said when I turned seven I could be a real camper and sleep in the cabins instead of at his house."

"Do you like sleeping in the cabin?"

"Oh yeah, it's fun. The girls are nice and they don't even get mad at me like Mom does when I read with my flashlight."

"What cabin are you in?"

"Pottawatami."

"That's the cabin I slept in when I was a camper."

"You slept in a cabin?"

"A long time ago. I was about your age when I first came, and then I came for many summers."

"Did you read a lot of books here?"

"Probably not as many as you because I liked to do things outside. But sometimes at home I would read with a flashlight after my mother turned off the lights. She always told me to not use the flashlight too. Maybe all moms are the same."

"My sister was a camper last year. She's two years older

and she's coming next week. It's her second year. She told me it would be a lot of fun."

"When you're done with your handprint in the craft room, would you like to make some bookmarks for all the books you read?"

"Yes. How many can I make? I brought three books with me."

"Three books for six days? That's almost a book every two days. Do you read that fast?"

"Sometimes, especially when I'm close to the end." Her smile shows a space where her two front teeth should have been.

It's hard not to hug her, so I do. "You could say we're special pals—Pottawatami pals who both like to read."

I leave her under the tree and head to my cabin, anxious to check my email to see if Parents Magazine has responded to my query for an article about how to prepare kids for a successful camp experience. With my laptop in hand, I go to the counselor lounge for Internet access.

The reply from Parents Magazine is there and I tap on the key.

> "Your query shows great promise and one we would have an interest in; however, a similar article is now appearing in our June issue. We are currently working on our holiday issue if you have any articles that would be relevant to that topic. If so, please send that query. In the future, we suggest you become familiar with our current issue to avoid duplication of topics."

Of course, I should have known that a camp article would be purchased four to five months before publication. I decide I will still write it now while the subject matter is available to me and submit again in December. Perhaps it's better not to have an acceptance and deadline. This way I can make notes each day and write the best articles at the end of the camp season.

I type in today's notes.

Don't worry if your child is not the outdoor type but would rather spend hours with a book instead of her friends swimming and canoeing. A good camp will provide time for campers to read and relax and not feel pressured to join each activity.

Or am I wrong? Should I have encouraged Emma to do more? Perhaps she would discover something she really loved as much as books. I can see that parenting is not easy, but then nothing worthwhile is. Not parenting, not relationships, not even friendship.

I picture my circle of friends for the past year. Or lack of. I haven't pursued any new girlfriends. Most of my friends had been at work or parts of a couple that Mike and I knew. Another sad part of divorce. Lose your husband and your lifestyle. People don't seem to be comfortable with you as a single person or maybe they don't know whose side to pick. In our case, most of our friends agreed that Mike had been a jerk, but being around them only reminded me that Mike and I were no longer together and soon I drifted away. Thank heavens for Amy, but I miss having girlfriends.

The counselor list comes to mind. I was supposed to call Lois back so I find the reunion folder and dial her number.

"Lois, it's Kim Douglas again. Sorry I missed you. Give me a call sometime after nine tonight. You know, after taps and lights out? Can't wait to catch up."

I leave my cell number and once again marvel at how

much things have changed since I was a camper. We had no contact with anyone outside of the campgrounds unless we received a letter from home. Perhaps it was best that way. We always said it was the perfect place to commit a murder. No one would ever know.

Pottawatami Cabin. Good Acres. Summer 1987

Dear Diary,

Mama's box of chocolate chip cookies came with a note. "Be sure to share with your cabin mates." She thinks that's the way to be popular.

Why would I give them anything when they are so mean to me? They heard me munching the cookies in bed after lights out and they started singing, "The ants go marching two by two. Hurrah, hurrah, They all jumped into Chubby's bed, hurrah, hurrah."

One Week Down

When the last car pulls out of the driveway Saturday at two o'clock, an hour later than it should have, Paul and I watch it make the downward curve, knowing we are now out of sight of their rearview mirror. We immediately turn to each other and grin.

"We did it. We survived the first week." We high-five each other.

Paul told the rest of the staff they could leave at one o'clock, which was when all the children should have been gone. No one objected and soon the only two cars in the parking lot are Paul's and mine.

Fifteen minutes ago, I was dog tired. Suddenly I have a sense of renewed energy. Twenty-four hours to myself. Well, twenty-two now.

"One week down, only nine to go." Paul seems elated. "Somehow, I don't think we're supposed to be this happy when they leave, are we?" he asks.

"Of course, you goon. That's in the best interests of the new kids coming on Sunday. We have to recharge our batteries for them. R & R."

"And that includes dinner for you and me—away from here. Remember Charley's? I owe you for... for...what do I owe you a dinner for?"

"I forgot. It was either too minor to remember or so humongous, one dinner will never cover it, so either way, let's just go. Maybe I'll even have an adult beverage." I continue. "We have a lot to celebrate. No one left before the end of the week, no one threw up on our sneakers, no pet snakes hid in the luggage, no accusations of petty theft."

"You mean those things normally happen?" Paul looks stricken as if he actually believes it. "None of the above were in the job description they showed me."

I can't tell if he's serious or just playing along. "Would anyone take this job if they told what really happens at camp? Come on, you know by now what kids are capable of."

"Oh yeah, but this twenty-four-hour thing is a little different than seeing them get on the school bus every day at three o'clock, isn't it?"

"I wouldn't know. Not having been a teacher or a parent."

"That's right, Miss Corporate Lady."

"Yes, and this Corporate Lady needs to make some real bucks now. Unfortunately, I have to keep paying rent on my apartment in Chicago even while I'm enjoying the luxuries of my penthouse suite here." I nod toward my cabin." I've got some writing to do before those little scumbags show up tomorrow. What time is dinner?"

"Seven?"

"Perfect. Meet you back here in the parking lot?"

"No date of mine is going to hang around a deserted parking lot at night. Don't the camp ghosts—all those disgruntled campers through the years—come out on Saturday night when they have the whole place to themselves? I'll come to your door and escort you to my limo."

My heart does a little skip. Our conversation is frivolous,

but it makes me feel young and silly. And special for the first time in a long time.

I sit down at my computer when my cell phone rings. It's Lois.

"So am I interrupting your Saturday quiet time? I bet you were napping, weren't you?"

"Not yet, but it's not a bad idea. First free time in a week. I feel like a kid out of school."

"Just imagine how those campers feel. Now that the shackles are off of them."

"Hey, what kind of place do you think we're running here? They have all kinds of freedom. I only had to tie one kid to her cot and that's because she didn't give me one darn cookie out of her care package. I could smell the chocolate at mail call."

"Gosh Kim, can you believe it's been so many years? You sound just the same—as witty as ever. I can't wait to see you. Do you want to come over tonight for dinner?"

"I'd love to but I actually have a date."

"A date? With who?"

"We have a lot of catching up to do. Let it suffice to say this is my first date since my divorce nine months ago. I'm kind of nervous. I haven't done this for a long time. In fact, I can't remember ever doing it. Mike and I just sort of evolved. Hardly dated anyone else at all."

"Well, darlin', you just go have a great time. When can I see you?"

"Why don't you come out to the campgrounds? I have free time from three to five each day. How about Tuesday? And speaking of marriage, why still your maiden name?"

"Professional reasons. Tell you later. See you Tuesday. I know the way."

First Date

I change my outfit three times. Charley's is a casual place in the woods, but it's Saturday night in the county seat. I want to wear something Paul hasn't seen me in yet, the camp shorts and tees every day. I finally settle on white capris and a sleeveless black shell with a scoop neck and a silver pendant. Dangling silver earrings and black sandals.

After washing and curling my hair, I pull it back leaving a few curly tendrils hanging beside each ear. Being in the sun more than usual is bringing out some highlights in my hair and my tan has deepened. I'm reaping the benefits of outdoor living.

I make sure all the tempera paint from the birdhouses we made is out from under my nails and I even paint my toenails since my last pedicure was long gone. I don't envision having one of those on a weekly basis here unless I make it an art project.

With fifteen minutes to go, I open my counselor reunion folder. I look at the group photo again and take another clean sheet of paper. I list the names again, this time with clear comments beside each one instead of the scribbles I had made while talking. Try google, send email, no phone. I get the creeps when writing dead beside Wendy and Sara.

A knock on the door jars me. I put my pencil down and stand, but decide to wait a minute before I answer. Don't act like it's a first date just because it is. That makes me smile and I keep smiling for Paul at the door. But I open it to find myself looking at JoAnna. It's the second time in a week she's startled me.

She says, "I just got back from the mall and saw your car still here. I thought you might like a little company." Before I can answer, she adds, "But it looks like you're going out."

Why do her words make me feel like I'm doing something wrong? Or is it that disapproving look she gives me?

"Actually, I am. Going out. To dinner, that is. But how nice of you to stop by. Maybe another time?"

"Of course."

She's turning to go as Paul comes up the path and sees her there. His eyes widen. I'm sure he's thinking like I did that all the staff have left. Evidently he didn't see her car which would have now been parked beside ours.

He says, "JoAnna, I thought you left for the night."

I sense his dilemma. Should he ask her to join us? I pray that he won't but he does.

"We're just going to get a bite. Would you like to join us?"

"That's so kind of you, but no thanks. I stopped at Café Court in the mall. I saw Kim's light and thought she might like a little company. You two run along and have a good time."

As she turns to leave, I step out of my cabin. Paul and I lock eyes. He shrugs and grimaces, as if to say, "I'm sorry."

I mouth the words, "It's okay."

Then he takes my elbow and leads me to his car. Before he opens the door, he leans down to whisper in my ear, "You look beautiful."

I slide into the seat, with mixed feelings. His touch and words have excited me, but the relief of JoAnna not coming with us is even greater.

As he puts the key in the ignition, I say, "I respect you for asking her to join us. Really. You're a nice person, Paul."

"Yeah, nice stupid person. What if she had said Yes? My gosh, we would have ended up talking about camp of all things on a Saturday night."

"I'm sure she has other interests in her life besides camp. And do you mean camp talk is off limits tonight?"

"Not really off-limits. Other things I'd rather talk about." He pats my knee.

"And what would those be?"

"You'll have to wait and see. Am I going the right way?" He has turned left out of the entrance and seems to be getting deeper into the woods.

"Maybe we were supposed to turn right."

There's nowhere to make a U-turn on the small two-lane road without going into the ditch, but when we come to a farmhouse driveway, we turn and head back past the campground entrance. The lampposts on the stone pillars are now lit as if it were the entrance to a private residence. There's a small brown sign saying Good Acres, but it's easy to miss if one weren't looking. If someone didn't know about camp, they would never suspect that little gravel road leads to a population of a hundred plus people and a little civilization unto itself. There's no indication of the life and drama that takes place up on the hill.

JoAnna there all alone. Doesn't she have anywhere to go on a Saturday night?

Charley's is crowded, but they say the wait would only be about ten minutes. Waylon Jennings is playing loudly in the bar, but I don't mind because Paul has to practically nuzzle my ear to be heard.

"Your hair smells good," he says. "And don't tell me it's

the lilacs here in this bar."

"I just hope I got all the paint and glue out. I forgot how boisterous seven-year-olds can be, but I certainly didn't want to stifle any budding artists. Oops, not supposed to talk shop."

"You can talk about anything you want," he whispers in my ear, his lips almost touching my skin. Then he touches my dangling earring and says, "Nice."

At this rate, I'm hoping our table will take forever, but in minutes they call his name.

The menu has lots of choices, so I ask, "Are you having steak?"

"At a steak house? That would be the way to go. How about you? They've got fish and ribs."

"I'm with you," I say. "What's our chances of getting any steak during the week?"

"Slim to none. And why would we give one hundred kids sharp knives?"

I say, "If you like fish, we'll have to ride out to the Beach Café. It's not that far. Do you remember it? Boned and buttered perch from Lake Michigan. Yum."

We chat about our college days, our first jobs. Paul tells me about his family. A brother in Seattle and a sister here with two nephews. Shows me pictures of them. Says he's going to try to get them to camp this year with the ten and eleven-year old boys. His mom and dad still live here but they're looking at a motor home to spend winters in Arizona near him and the sun.

He's wearing a pair of khaki Dockers and a crisp white shirt which makes his tan seem even more striking. "So tell me how you got that white shirt looking so good. You have some little camper slaving away over a hot iron—-the one you made fun of me for bringing."

"I discovered a cleaners right next to the bank on Hwy

41. Six days of camp tees is enough—even for a guy."

By the time our dessert comes, we inevitably slip into camp talk, but nothing serious.

"I'm bending the rules a bit next week and letting Herb's granddaughter return for a second week since her sister, Heather, is coming. It should be fine even though she'll be younger than the others. Her sister will look out for her."

"Oh, you mean Emma, our little bookworm?"

"Yes, that would be her. The swimming pool is the only place she doesn't have her book saddled to her hip. By the way, she told me she loves her arts-and-crafts teacher. The one who says it's okay to read a lot."

"I wonder if I did the right thing to praise her reading. Should have probably encouraged her to play tennis or something outdoors."

"Why?"

"I don't know. Balance in her life and all that."

"If she's happy, and it's not bothering anyone, I don't see anything wrong with it."

"How about you?" I ask. "Do you have balance in your life? Back home, I mean."

"I suppose I do. Working, coaching. I play golf with the same foursome each week. Good guys except they're all married. I feel kind of envious when they talk about their kids."

"Well, now you have a hundred cute kids of your own. You'll have lots of pictures to take home."

"How about you? Did you want to have a family?"

"Sure, but maybe we got too caught up in our careers and it never seemed like a good time to have a baby. Now I probably never will."

"Why do you say that?" He looks surprised.

"I don't know how long it's going to take me to trust anyone again—you know, enough to get married. By that time, it might be too late. Sounds like we're back to biology class again." I smile, trying to steer the conversation back to something light.

He smiles. "Well, we'll just have to see about that. Maybe a crash course could speed things up."

I'm all for accelerated learning.

When we return to the campgrounds, there's a light on in Herb's house, but other than that, the grounds are dark and quiet. As we round the bend to the Lodge, we see a light in JoAnna's cabin, but the outdoor beacon is off. Guess she doesn't expect any sleepwalkers on Saturday night. Her car and mine are the only ones parked in the lot.

The Porch Swing

The summer evening temperature is perfect. Only a sliver of moon and the stars are extra bright with no city lights to dim them.

"It's really too nice to go in, isn't it?" Paul asks.

"Yes, I agree. Too nice to go in." And too nice to be alone.

We walk to the front porch and sit on one of the wooden porch swings, which creaks with each movement.

"Shh, you're drowning out the crickets and cicadas," he says.

"You're the one who's rocking. Sit still." I spank his hand which is lying between us on the swing.

He takes my hand and holds it in his, running his fingers gently over the back of it. How can something so simple arouse me so much? Am I so starved for affection or am I just touched by his tenderness?

We sit that way for some time, neither of us saying a word. Now his index finger is making little circles on the back of my hand and up my arm. Tingles travel all the way up to my scalp. Is this some kind of acupuncture foreplay?

"Okay, Kim, I'm going to say it again. I'm really glad you're here. I was excited about this job even before I knew you would be here, but now it's more…more than I hoped for."

"Oh? What did you hope for?"

"A summer full of life and people. You know, a family of sorts."

"I feel the same way. It's nice to be around people all day. And night. I was starting to go batty living the hermit life in my condo and didn't even realize it." I chuckle. "We act like we can't wait for the campers to leave, but it's easy to get attached to them. Now, granted, it's only the first week. By week ten, I'll be helping them pack their bags." I cover his hand with mine. "And I haven't told you that I'm glad to be here too. Wasn't really sure how it would turn out."

"Life's a gamble, isn't it? We make choices, take chances. No guarantees. Sometimes they work; sometimes they don't. I told myself I could stand anything for ten weeks. The biggest regret I might have is by the time I figure out how to improve on the system here, the summer will be over."

"Well, there's always next year…and the next and the next."

"This would be a terrific job for a family. What a great place for children to spend the summer," he says.

If he keeps doing that magic swirly thing with his fingers, we could be one step closer to making that family. Then to make matters worse, and much better at the same time, his fingers go to the back of my neck and make little circles there.

"I like those little curls." He gently pulls one of the tendrils.

Not trusting myself to say something coherent, I return to our original conversation. "Yes, some lucky kids would get to spend ten weeks at camp—and sleep in the air-conditioned director's cabin."

"What a great way to make every other kid hate them. If my nephews come, no special attention."

"Speaking of hate, did you see any signs of cruel and unusual punishment this week? Any revolts in the cabins?"

"None that I know of. I'm no expert, but I imagine everyone is trying so hard the first week. Problems may surface later when the counselors let their guard down a bit. They're human after all," he says.

"And because counselors are human, we'll have the inevitable summer romances between them. Put all these hormones together for ten weeks, it's bound to happen. If you're ever up in the middle of the night, you might check out the third floor of the Lodge. It was a popular necking spot."

"Oh, speaking from experience?"

"Of course not. I wouldn't leave my little charges alone in the middle of the night. It's not that I was such a goody two shoes. I was too afraid that Murphy's Law would kick in. Even if I only tried to sneak out once, it would have been my luck that was the night a camper had the nightmare of all nightmares or wet the bed or something equally gross."

I roll my eyes. "That happened to one of the counselors. She snuck up there to meet the lifeguard, and sure enough, her cabin went into a panic when they discovered she was gone. Woke up the whole camp."

"Good to know," he said.

"There were those weeks you really liked some kids more than others. You know, the chemistry of it all, how they gelled. But even on the worst weeks when I couldn't wait for Saturday to arrive, I sometimes missed the little rebels when they left.

"Let me re-phrase that. Maybe for ten minutes. Sometimes, I missed the troublemakers the most. They were so darn creative, they found more ways to bend the rules."

Now Paul is twirling a piece of my hair in his fingers. If it goes any further, I could be a lost cause and my vulnerable self isn't ready to get lost in anyone yet.

I say, "Well, this swing is rocking me to sleep. I imagine you're beat too. You've been going nonstop, and I bet you another dinner you're spending a lot of hours on paperwork in the evening, aren't you?"

"Bets are off. But I'd love to have dinner again. How about that fish place? Next Saturday?"

"Can we slip away without getting caught this time?"

"Maybe we should start earlier? Like noon?"

"Yeah, let's beat the kids out of the gate, I say.

"Should we lock the gates at one o'clock like the brochure says and leave those kids sitting outside on their luggage? When the parents pull up, they'll realize we're not their weekend babysitters."

"Good for the parents, bad for the kids. Tempting though. Or we lock the gates and say all leftover kids have been impounded. Like when they tow your car at the airport."

"Oh great, then we're stuck with them all weekend. I don't think so."

I chuckle. "If the parents could hear us now, they'd never leave them here at all."

He walks me to my door. When I turn to say goodnight, he lifts my chin and kisses the tip of my nose and then brushes his lips softly on my cheek. It seems a perfect way to end the evening, and I'm glad I didn't pucker up a real kiss that wasn't in his plan.

He holds me close to him for just a minute and I don't resist a bit. It's a good fit.

Then he whispers in my ear, "Nice and easy, Kim. Let's take it nice and easy. You're still sorting things out. I don't want to rush you."

My mind is saying, Rush me, rush me. Aloud, I say, "That's very sweet, Paul. You're right. I don't want to make another mistake."

"Oh, Mike's the one who made the mistake. Letting you go was a very big mistake. See you tomorrow. Sleep tight."

"Thanks for dinner and you sleep good too. You did a great job this week."

He waits for me to open the door and then just as he turns to go, he says, "Oh, by the way, I'd like to see a better profit on those sweatshirts tomorrow in the camp store. I thought you had a big career in advertising. Let's move that stuff."

"I'll work out a big ad campaign first thing in the morning. Something real original. Like buy one, get one free?"

He laughs and walks away. I close the door behind me and stand with my back to the door, savoring the moment. Kinda glad Mari is gone tonight so I can keep our date private for now.

I undress and put on my extra-large camp tee shirt—the one I sleep in. Usually I read but decide I'm too sleepy. When I turn off the lamp at my desk, I notice my open folder with the counselor reunion names. The old group photo is lying on top. Funny, but I thought I left the sheet with the ten names and my notes on top. In fact, I'm sure of it because I'd just finished the last note when the knock came, and I jumped up. I don't remember reshuffling my papers. I pick up the nine by twelve-inch photo and see my worksheet with notes underneath it.

Has someone been in my cabin? I didn't lock my door when I left. The confusion with JoAnna and all. Mari and I didn't lock our door all week. We agreed that we didn't want to be saddled with keys each day. It just never occurred to us that it wouldn't be safe or private. Now, I go to the door and slide the little wooden dead bolt across the top and turn the key in the lock where it has been since the day we moved in. No one's at the camp tonight except JoAnna and Herb. Surely they wouldn't have come in. Had any of the counselors returned? There were no other cars in the driveway.

I'm tired. I'll think about it in the morning. I switch off the light and climb under the covers, thinking how nice Paul's touch was on the swing.

The next morning, a strange dream is still fresh in my mind. I was sitting on the porch swing with Paul. On the swing facing us at the other end of the porch sat Mike and B.B. They were kissing passionately, and their swing kept going faster and faster until it fell off its hooks with them on top of each other.

Paul kept whispering to me, "It's okay. We're going nice and slow. You won't fall off."

Lois

Lois puts her hands on my shoulders the way a mother looks at a child when she sends them off to their first day of school. Am I properly dressed?

"Oh, my gosh, look at you." she says. "I should have known you'd look great. You could have prepared me so I would at least have worn my Spanx."

This is after she has given me a hug that nearly crushes me. Lois has always been a big girl, but not fat. Now she is probably carrying an extra twenty pounds on her large frame, but it seems to be evenly distributed.

Her weight doesn't have a negative effect on her self-esteem as she wears bright orange capris with a fuchsia and orange striped top. The stripes are even horizontal which everyone knows is a no-no for heavy women, but it's almost as if she wants to flaunt her size. Her outfit screams Look at me. Her face is lovely enough to be a Lane Bryant model. Just a touch of eye makeup, blush and a striking, glossy tangerine lip color.

I am unprepared for the gush of feeling I have for Lois at the moment. Her hug and smile show unconditional joy to see me. It's like a drug. A big shot of dopamine goes straight to my head, or in this case, my heart.

"Lois, I can't tell you how good it is to see you. Why did we wait so long?"

"Well, girl you tell me. I'm not the one who disappeared to the big city. I heard you were some high-powered ad person. Is that true? And now a camp counselor? This doesn't make sense. I mean it's nice to see you here, but—"

"It didn't make sense to me either when my life fell apart. I'm taking a little time off before I get back on track." I take her by the hand. "Come on in, or do you want to explore the campgrounds first for old times' sake?"

"I want to explore you first. Then you can give me the tour. I can't believe coming through those gates how nothing has changed, has it? It's like stepping back in time."

"Exactly. It's amazing how the rest of the world has changed, and Good Acres stays hidden here frozen in time. What can I get you? Coffee, soda, iced tea?"

"Iced tea sounds good. You have a kitchen in here?" Lois looks around my one-room cabin.

"Are you kidding? A bed, a chair, and yes, indoor plumbing—all my own." I point to the closet. "Toity and shower. I couldn't have done it otherwise. This is about as 'roughing it' as I'm willing to do. Come on, we'll go up to the Lodge kitchen. I now have staff privileges."

"You get to cross the forbidden line of the kitchen door? This job is just full of perks, isn't it?"

We walk across the driveway to the back door of the Lodge, but then I say, "Let's go in through the front door, the way you remember it, okay?" We walk around to the front, climb the stairs to the porch and enter through the heavy double knotty-pine doors.

When she steps inside, Lois stops and lets out a big "Oh, my gosh." She says, "I can't believe how good it feels to see this again. Your reunion idea is great." She heads directly to the table in the left corner.

"This was my cabin's table. Iroquois. I'm sure I got all the special-needs kids or something. Every week my centerpiece was the most hideous. I wanted to gag at each meal. But as you can see—" she spreads her hands across her waist, "I seemed to keep it all down."

We go into the kitchen and I open the door of the large stainless-steel refrigerator. Lois ambles around looking at everything. "It's amazing how many kids this place has fed through the years."

I pour the tea. "A hundred kids plus staff for ten weeks, for over sixty years now. Yes, that's a lot of mac and cheese."

"How's the food?"

"Actually good. And the cooks are adorable—they must have degrees in psychology or something. Just the other day, a little skinny girl, Rachael, ahead of me in line, asked if the meal was kosher, and Edna, the head cook, just smiled and said, 'Of course, honey. You eat all you can. It's all kosher.'"

Just then a few counselors come in and sit at one of the tables, laughing.

"Come on, let's go back to my cabin. Before you leave though, we'll come back through here so I can show you the scrapbooks. Someone has kept an amazing history of each year. You'll see yourself in a lot of photos."

We take our iced teas back to my cabin. I sit cross-legged on my bed and she sits on the one chair I use at my desk. I tell Lois my sad marriage saga, and she listens intently and asks just the right questions until I find myself pouring out every awful feeling I've had in the last six months.

I even tell her what I haven't told anyone else—not even Amy. The horrible moment when I came home unexpectedly and found Mike in our bed with Bimbo. She was naked and straddled over Mike, her huge breasts dangling just inches from his face.

"Sometimes I keep playing that scene over and over. It comes to me at the strangest times. I just want to erase it from my memory. Wish there was such a thing as selective amnesia." Finally, I say, "Okay enough of me. What have you been doing?"

She smiles sheepishly. "You know how I always loved to solve everyone's problems and give advice?"

"Oh no, don't tell me you're the new Ann Landers. Am I going to read my awful story in tomorrow's paper?"

"No actually, I'm bound to patient privacy."

"What? You're a doctor?"

"A psychologist actually. That's why I use my maiden name. Started my practice with it and didn't want to change."

"Are you billing me for this talk?"

"You bet. Too bad there's no couch in here. Since you didn't actually lie down, I'll give you a discount."

"Lois, that's amazing. No wonder it was so easy to talk to you. You knew all the questions to ask. Which buttons to push."

"That has nothing to do with my degree, Kim. I've always liked you. You were the most popular girl in camp and the cutest, but you never acted like it. Your head was on so straight all the time. Although you were in on all the pranks, you were more sensitive than most of us who got caught up in groupthink. Remember, you were the one who said we had to stop being so mean to Patty."

"Who was Patty?"

"You forgot? You know, Fatty Patty and then she became Pee-Pee Pat when Sara discovered that she wet the bed. Sara hung her sheets on the clothesline outside."

Something about the words sheets and Sara together trigger a nagging thought. What did her aunt tell me about her death?

I say to Lois, "Oh my gosh, I forgot all about that. It all blends together after so many years. We have to go through those albums again."

"Let's see, There were three or four of us who were campers in Pottawatami and then we became counselors at the same time years later," Lois says,

I stand to grab the folder beside the computer and pull the list of names. "Here's a list of the counselors our last year together." I hand my original list to Lois, the one without my comments.

Lois studies it. "Oh yeah, here we go. There were Wendy, Sara, Trish, you and me. We were all in Pottawatami as campers. Remember, we were all jealous when you got to be the counselor to Pottawatami, so you didn't have to learn any new stupid tribe songs."

I was hardly listening to Lois anymore. A cold chill spiraled up my spine as I reached for the second list where I was making comments for each girl she had called. Beside Wendy's name: Dead. Beside Sara's name: Dead. Both counselors had been campers in Pottawatami with Lois and me.

"There's something a little strange here. Have you kept in touch with any of these counselors?"

Lois studies the list. "At first I did. Those of us who were in the area. But I've been gone for several years myself. We just moved back last year. Wanted to raise the kids near the grandparents."

"Do you know what's happened to Wendy and Sara?"

"I read about Wendy's accident. Something about a snakebite. I couldn't believe it."

"Do you know about Sara?"

"Know what?"

"She was strangled. With a bed sheet."

"How do you know this?"

"I talked to her aunt. The parents left the area after it happened. Moved to Florida. I was going to Google both Wendy and Sara to get the whole stories, but I got so freaked out. I wanted to keep calling the others and then camp got under way. Frankly, I've sort of blocked it out."

"This is too weird. It's creeping me out. Who else have you called?"

I handed her the list. "I was hoping you might know some of their last names if they married. I'm running into a few dead ends."

"Dead end is right. Oops, sorry about that. Not funny."

She reads aloud, "Wendy Hansen—died of snakebite."

Nancy Morris—living on west coast. Sent email nanmor@aol.com.

Barb Bailey—left message.

Sara Scordoto—died of strangulation.

Trish Whipple-daughter Betsy. Phone: 219-555-8890

Laurie Mayer-no contact

Kathy Knoles-no contact

Lois Betka-success! phone: 219-555-8765

Kim Douglas.

"What do you think, Lois? Is it just a strange coincidence that two of our team have died so young?'

"Stranger things have happened. I'd like to know what Laurie and Kathy are doing now. Can I keep this list? I have more time and resources at home than you do here. I'm surprised your cell even works in this wilderness."

"Let's go to the director's office. I can make a copy off his fax machine. He's the guy I went to high school with. The one who recruited me at my ten-year reunion."

Go To A Happy Place

We knock on Paul's door and hear "Come in."

Seated at his desk, phone to his ear, he waves us in and holds up one finger while winking at me. In khaki camp shorts and a black polo shirt with the inevitable whistle, he looks like he could be on the cover of Outdoor Living. It's the first time I've seen him with glasses since high school, but these are definitely not the nerdy black frames with tape in the middle. Stylish tortoise shell devoid of coke bottles frame his soft brown eyes.

I feel a little tug at my chest watching his hand make notes as he speaks on the phone. The dark hair on the back of his hand reminds me of his fingers circling the back of my neck the other night on the swing. I'm blushing.

I catch Lois eyeing me and know I have been found out. She smiles and rolls her eyes.

"You got some 'splaining to do Lucy," she whispers.

I glare at her, willing her to stop talking

"You've been holding out on your doctor. That isn't nice, now is it?"

"Later," I say.

Paul hangs up and turns to us.

"Paul, I'd like you to meet my friend, Lois. We were counselors together. You know, back in the Dark Ages."

Paul reaches out his hand "Great to meet you. Looking for a summer job?"

"I told you that would happen," I say to her.

I turn to Paul. "Actually, she'd be a great addition. She's a psychologist."

"Just what this place needs. Can you come back in week ten? We'll all be crazy by then."

Lois picks right up on it. "Probably five weeks would be more like it."

Paul laughs while making eye contact with me.

"Can we make a quick copy off your fax? Just one page."

He waves me toward the fax and turns to Lois, "Can you stay and have dinner with us? There's always one more serving of whatever we're having."

"And what would that be?"

He glances at the calendar on the wall above his desk. "If it's Tuesday, must be spaghetti and meatballs."

"Sounds good, but I have my own little set of campers waiting for me at home."

"Will they be joining us this summer? No, you're too young to have camp-age kids."

Lois looks flattered. "Oh, you silver-tongue orator you. Actually, I'm old enough, but they're not. Just four and five. A few more years and I'll be driving through those Sunday gates at noon."

I pipe in. "And I hope you're not one of those who waits till the last minute on Saturday to pick up. You'd better be here by noon or those kids are off to Neverland." I try to sound tough.

"Whoa, tight ship you're running here. Good try, Kim, but you can't fool me. You've haven't changed. You'd have them sitting on your lap with milk and cookies. Paul, you've probably figured her out by now, haven't you?"

He glances at me. "I'm trying to. Every chance I get."

"Thanks, Paul. See you later," I say as the fax shoots out the copy.

"Nice to meet you, Lois. Come back anytime."

As we step out of Paul's cabin, I take Lois by the arm, pretending to be mad. "And what was that figuring her out all about?"

"Just wanted to be sure he knew how nice you are," Lois smiles sheepishly.

"Talk about nice. Isn't he cute? Okay, Doc, is it too soon? Is it a rebound thing with me?"

"Darling, if he makes you feel like a woman again, you go for it. Give it all you've got and get back in the human race. This is not a dress rehearsal for life. Live it now. As far as we know, it's the only chance we've got."

Lois's words should have given me a lift, permission to live and love again, but instead Wendy and Sara come to mind. No more chances. Was it Shakespeare? Life is but a play—we are all actors on the stage…or something like that. Their performance is over.

"Do you have time to see the albums?"

"Gosh, I'd love to, but I've got to run. I told my mom I'd pick up the kids by six. She and Dad are doing their ballroom dancing thing on Tuesdays."

"Ballroom dancing? That's great."

"We tease them about it, but it's been amazing. Keeps them in shape. Causes some problems though. Mom wants to enter the competitions, but Dad won't practice. She tells him, 'You practice your golf swing for hours at that driving range. Why won't you practice dance?' He says, 'Dancing is supposed to be fun. Golf is serious.' Go figure. Who would have thought at their age they'd be competing for anything but rocking chairs?"

"Lois, you're bad. I forgot how sick your humor was."

"Well, in my profession, if you can't laugh about life's

problems, you're going to be in deep trouble. Some ugly stuff out there."

So I found out.

I walk Lois to her car, a metallic blue BMW.

"Nice car," I say. "People are willing to pay big bucks to get their heads on straight, aren't they?

"Kim, I usually don't dish out advice to friends, but one thing I can tell you is this. It seems you've still got some work to do with this anger. It's going to take a little time, but try not to play the bedroom scene over and over in your mind. You know, Mike and what's her face? As you play it over and over, you keep the anger and frustration fresh. That constant replay in one's head—that picture—is what makes people display hostile behavior many years after the event that hurt them so much. If it comes into your mind, turn it off or switch channels. Use your inner remote control and go to a happy place. That hunk in the director's cabin might be a good place to visit."

She smiles and hugs me.

This time I hug her twice as hard and feel the tears smarting my eyes. "Lois, I can't tell you what this means to me. Seeing you again. Reminding me of the person I used to be. And now this good free advice."

"Who said it was free?" She laughs and gets in her car.

"Let me know what you find on the list," I say.

As she drives off, the dinner bell rings. Campers pour out of their cabins and run up the hill. This group has been here two nights now and friendships are forming. Nine and ten-year old girls like to hold hands, and many of them come up the hill hanging onto each other, giggling and whispering.

Tomorrow I'll have my camera on the porch and capture them on the hill. It will give my camp article a new twist. Friendships we form away from home can last a lifetime.

Lois is proof of that.

Pottawatami Cabin Good Acres. 1987
Dear Diary,

Mealtimes and bedtimes are the worst. The loneliest. When the dinner bell rings and everyone climbs the hill to the Lodge, my cabin-mates walk with their arms joined at the elbows and sometimes they're singing. I plod up alone behind them, usually panting by the time I get to the top.

I get so mad at Mama. It's her fault I'm fat and her fault that I'm here. But I'll never tell her what happened. She'll go on and on with one of her motivational sayings. "You must do what you fear." Or her favorite Eleanor Roosevelt one. "No one can make you feel inferior without your consent." Well, Eleanor never had to go to Good Acres Camp.

At last the week if over. I can't stand to watch them all saying good-bye and mushy things like, "It was the best week of my life." Some are even crying. They're making a list of phone numbers and addresses. My name's not on it, but I snatched a copy. It will come in handy when I decide how to get even.

Then they'll have something to cry about.

Friendships

The next evening I'm waiting on the stoop of the front porch for the dinner bell to ring. I have my camera in hand with the telephoto lens in place. I don't want the campers to know they're being photographed. I want to capture them spontaneously, talking to each other—the giggling, the affection.

JoAnna comes up the hill and sits beside me. I'm glad to see her. I'd meant to try to spend some time with her this week, still feeling bad about turning down her Saturday night invitation.

"Are you the official photographer this year?" JoAnna asks.

"No, just doing some freelance work. Thought I'd capture some of this camp life to put above my computer as I write. It helps to have a visual sometimes."

"Good idea. Anything special you're looking for?"

"I like to see the friendships that are forming. See how they hold hands and wrap their arms around each other's waists. It's like some unwritten code."

"How about those kids walking up alone? Are you going to tell their story too?"

"Oh, there's Emma. She's alone, but not really. She's always got her best friend with her—an open book."

Emma almost stumbles into a group ahead of her as she

tries to read and walk."

"Watch where you're going, four eyes," I hear someone say.

Emma looks up but doesn't seem fazed by the remark. Then she spots me and runs toward me. "I finished The Mystery of the Old Clock. It was a good one. Do you remember what happened?"

"No and don't tell me. I might want to read it again."

"I'm reading the second one now." She holds up The Hidden Staircase.

"Hello, Nurse JoAnna," Emma says politely and walks into the Lodge.

"Name-calling doesn't seem to affect her self-esteem, does it?" I comment.

"Well, you know what they say. 'No one can make you feel inferior without your consent.'"

"Great quote. Who said that?"

"I believe it was Eleanor Roosevelt. You know she knew about the president's affaires but refused to be intimidated."

I say, "If anyone had a right to feel rejected, it would have been her." Now there's a positive tape I should be playing in my head. One that says I'm not giving my consent.

We get up to walk in.

I say, "Let's see. Wednesday. Must be chicken fingers and fries. Would you like to sit together for dinner?" Still trying to make up for Saturday night.

"I'd like that," JoAnna says.

One Fire Too Many

It's the end of the second week. We are all returning from the Friday night bonfire and closing ceremony. Campers again walk single file, following one another closely with their flashlights pointing to the ground to light the way. We experienced the thrill of fire from the gods and sang our favorite camp songs.

The walk back to the cabins is somber as the campers become aware it's their last night together and the week has passed too quickly. As usual, there is even some sobbing from the drama queens. The counselors know the campers will stay up late, and they have little leverage to convince them otherwise. The next morning is only breakfast, packing and waiting for the parents.

I'm at the head of the line leading the entourage out of the woods. Counselors are dispersed throughout the line with their little charges to keep them moving. Like last week, Paul and the maintenance boys will be the last ones out to make sure the fire is doused.

As I near the clearing, I smell fire again and think it's strange that the smell of the bonfire has carried so far. As we get closer to the opening, the smell becomes stronger rather than fading. Something isn't right.

As soon as we reach the clearing, indeed something is

very wrong. Off to my right, flames shoot high in the air. Where are they coming from? It's one of the cabins. The one on the far right. It's Pottawatami. Engulfed in flames.

I race toward the fire, and soon the entire line is running behind me. I don't have my cell phone with me. I shout to Mari who's a few feet behind me, "Keep the campers away from the fire. Lead the line to the playground. I'm going for help."

The nurse's station has to be the closest phone. Surely JoAnna has called. She didn't come to the bonfire because she had two sick campers.

I have to make sure no one was in the cabin, but as I run past Pottawatami, the heat of the flames makes me realize it would be crazy to try to get near it. Thank goodness every camper is required to attend the closing ceremony unless they're with the nurse.

I run to the nurse's cabin and find JoAnna sitting on the stoop of her cabin watching the flames. She appears unusually calm.

She says, "I called the fire department. As soon as I saw the flames." Her voice reminds me of a robot's. She hardly looks at me, but seems to be looking beyond me at the burning cabin, mesmerized by the flames.

"Are you sure there's no one in the cabin?" I ask.

"Aren't all the campers required to go to the bonfire? Except the two I have here in bed."

"Yes, but we have to be sure."

I run back to the cabin, getting as close as the heat of the flames would allow. Where are the firemen? How far do they have to come? The sirens resound at the same time I see Paul running toward me. By this time word must have spread back to him at the clearing.

"My God, how did this happen?" We have to go in and make sure no one's in there."

"Paul, no, it's not safe. The firemen are on the way."

Then I see the reflection of the fire truck lights coming up the gravel path. Where will they connect to water? What emergency provisions are in place for something like this?

We both watch as the truck stops briefly on the concrete flagpole area next to the Lodge. In just a few minutes, the truck is coming down the grassy area with a hose uncoiling from the side of the truck. It seems to be attached to something back near the flagpole. Will it be long enough?

They drive as far as the hose will allow them and several firemen jump off the truck with axes and fire extinguishers. Two others blast the hose, and fortunately the spray is reaching the cabin.

A fireman says to Paul, "No use trying to go in until we can get some of those flames down. This old wood will be ashes and cinder in no time."

Paul calls to me, "Kim, go back to the playground area. Line up all the campers from Pottawatami. Make sure they're all accounted for. Hurry."

I run as fast as I can and call for Jordan, the Pottawatami counselor, as soon as I reach the playground. The campers are huddled together, most of them crying while the counselors and instructors try to calm them.

"Jordan, count your campers. Make sure they're all here."

"Girls, line up here." She does a quick count. "Yes, everyone's here," she shouts back to me.

In the small group gathered around Jordan, one little camper is almost hysterical. At first I don't recognize her in the dark, and then I realize it's Emma's older sister, Heather.

Heather is shouting, "Where's Emma? She didn't go to the campfire. She wanted to finish her book. What if she's in the cabin? What if she's in the burning cabin? I have to go find Emma."

"No, Heather," Jordan says. "You stay with me. Emma's safe. She said she was going to go to your grandfather's house. That's what she told me."

Heather is crying so hard we can hardly understand her.

"But when we left for the campfire, she was still on the bed reading. When Emma has her nose in a book, she forgets everything else. What if she was still reading there? I have to go."

Heather breaks away from Jordan and begins running. I run after her. "Jordan, stay here with the other girls."

"Heather, wait, I'm coming with you. We'll find Emma."

When we got closer to the fire it seems to be diminishing, but the fireman won't let us near the cabin. "Stand back."

I shout in the face of the fireman pushing us back. "One of the girls might have been left behind. Please, please can someone see if she's in there?"

Herb, where's Herb? He'll know if Emma is at the house or not?

I survey people gathered. No sign of Herb. He must have had to open the gate to let the fireman in. "Paul, we have to find Herb. Emma's missing. She might be in the cabin if she's not with Herb."

"My God," Paul runs toward the burning cabin.

A fireman chases and yanks him back. "What? Are you crazy? No one's going in there, buddy."

"I'm responsible. I have to find Emma." Paul looks like a raged animal.

The flames are dying down. We can see what is left. Just the steel frames of the bunks. Nothing else remains. Everything is charred. Gone.

"We'll be walking through it in just a minute. Stay back. Don't get any closer. Do you hear me?" He is speaking directly to Paul, Heather, and me.

Just as he moves toward the cabin to confirm our worst

fears, we hear a familiar voice behind us.

It's Herb. "That was some spectacle. I could see those flames back from the road."

We turn and all of us cry with relief. Holding Herb's hand, a book in the other, is little Emma.

"Grandpa, the cabin is all gone. I'm glad I was at your house."

Heather comes running to Emma, sobbing, and Herb put his arms around both the girls. In the group hug, Emma pats Heather's back. "It's okay, Heather. They'll build another cabin. Won't they, Grandpa?"

"I don't care about the cabin, you ninny. I thought you were in it. I was so scared," Heather says.

"Me? I told you I was going to Grandpa's."

"But I left you there reading on the bed."

"I just wanted to finish the chapter. Then I walked to the Lodge to meet Grandpa. I saw his truck in the driveway waiting for me."

Paul and I run to each other.

"Thank God, she's safe." He holds me tightly and I can't stop the tears. "It's okay. It's okay. It's going to be alright."

"Let's get all kids up to the Lodge. We need to calm everyone down before bedtime. Thank goodness it didn't jump to the other cabins."

I go to the playground and spread the word to the counselors and instructors. "No one is hurt. Everyone up to the Lodge."

Unfortunately, the clothes and possessions of the Pottawatami campers are lost. Some of them are crying about their destroyed arts and crafts projects. Luckily, most of them are wearing the moccasins and head feathers they had made during the week.

Paul says, "Kim, go into the store and gather up some tee-shirts and sweatshirts. Don't we have nighties too?

That's the least we can do. Better yet, take them in with you. Have each of them pick out three items that fit them."

"Mari, go down to the canteen and bring up as many ice cream sandwiches as we have. Candy bars too."

I say, "Paul, I hate to put a damper on your party, but do they need all that sugar before bedtime?"

"No one's going to bed for hours, Kim. We've got to turn this into something positive so they don't go home scared to death."

The cooks must have heard the fire truck and are now in the kitchen in their chenille robes. Edna has big pink curlers in her hair and Mabel is adjusting her hair net while she recites Luke 10:19. …nothing will injure you.

"Edna, some hot chocolate might be nice. Can we whip up a big batch of it?" Paul asks.

"You bet. And I've got marshmallows too. They could use a little sugar after all this excitement."

Paul's smug look makes me smile, my first since the fire. As if he can't resist, he says, "See, sugar is a good thing in a crisis."

I know when I'm outnumbered and give it up. The girls are wound as tight as three-day clocks right now. What's a little more stimulation?

While the kids are gorging on candy, the fire chief comes in and says the fire is completely out. They'll return in the morning to uncover the cause of the blaze.

Paul asks the chief if he would say a few words to the kids to assure them that they are safe.

Somehow we get through the night. Courtney, the drama coach, has her resources and the foresight to start a group activity. She claps her hands on her knees and starts chanting, "We're Going on a Bear Hunt." The girls repeat the refrain with her as they pantomime the actions. When they finish, we dim the lights and start singing Climbing

Jacob's Ladder and I can feel the tension in the room dissolving. Some of the girls are nodding their heads and slightly dozing off.

At the end of the song, each counselor gathers their ten charges and walks down the hill with their flashlights. Jordan's girls will sleep in the Lodge. She asks if someone could take a group picture of the Pottawatami girls since most of them would have lost their cameras in the fire.

"Good thinking, Jordan," I say as I run to my cabin to get mine. We arrange them standing in two rows for the photo and then we spread out the army blankets I found in the storage closet. We roll up sweatshirts from the store for pillows. Eight in a row on the stage. Jordan is going to sleep in the middle of them, four on each side. Heather and Emma decide to sleep at Grandpa's house.

"Do you want me to stay here with you?" I ask Jordan.

"That might be a good idea."

"I'm staying too," Paul says.

"Boys at our slumber party? No way." I try to make the campers laugh and it works as several of them giggle.

The girls settle in and I hear a soft melodic voice. Jordan is singing a lullaby. Her sweet voice brings tears to my eyes. I know Jordan will not forget this night and I won't either.

"Good-night, Jordan," I whisper when she finishes singing.

Then a chorus of good-nights is heard, sounding like the Waltons' "Good-night John-Boy."

"Good-night, Kim," Jordan is the last to answer in a sleepy voice.

As I go to my cabin to get a pillow and blanket for myself, I meet JoAnna on the Lodge steps.

"I came up to get my two patients a little bedtime snack," she says.

Then under the porch light I notice that her face seems

radiant.

She adds with a smile, "That was some fire, wasn't it?"

Sweet Dreams

Paul peeks his head into the Lodge and motions for me to come to him. I get up quietly and tiptoe to the front porch where he's headed.

"Kim, I need to talk and unwind for a few minutes. I can't believe this happened. Thank God, no one was hurt, but what a scare. What a horrible and frightening thing for the little girls to see. I feel terrible."

"It's not your fault, Paul. You can't be everywhere. Someone probably left a candle burning or something."

"They had candles in the cabins?"

"Well, not supposed to, but who knows? It had to be something like that. Maybe someone had matches."

"Hope the firemen don't tell us we have a little arsonist among us. Now I have to figure out where to put the ten girls who would have been in Pottawatami next week."

"How about the second crafts cabin. I don't need two cabins for crafts. We're working outside most of the time anyway. The extra cabin is mostly storage for the paints and stuff."

"I could have understood it if the craft cabin burned down. We'd better make sure tomorrow that there's nothing flammable in there."

"Here you were worried about the fire at the clearing with the toilet paper escapade. Guess we were worrying about the wrong place."

"I'd better let you get some sleep," he says finally. When we stand up, I can't resist putting my arms around his waist and pulling him close to me.

"Paul, it's going to be alright."

He holds on tightly, looks down at me and smiles tenderly. "I'm so glad you're here. Have I told you lately?" The phrase has become our private joke, and in spite of how tired I am, it makes me smile.

"No, not lately. First time today. I was beginning to wonder if I'd done something wrong. Now please try to sleep. You're going to need it."

When I return to the row of campers, they all seem to be asleep, including Jordan. They're cuddled close together and I want to take one last picture. It could be something I'd send each of them later since they'd lost so much. I was hoping the flash won't wake them. They look too precious not to take it. As soon as the flash goes off, I see some movement out of the corner of my eye and notice that JoAnna has slipped back into the Lodge.

"How are the two little patients?" I ask her.

"Their fevers just broke. Well, only one had a fever. The other was sympathy pains. They wanted to spend their last night with friends in their cabin so I walked them back there."

"You missed the hot chocolate and candy fest. I thought they'd all be on a sugar high, but Courtney got them calmed down. Even the Pottawatami bunch." I nod to the stage.

JoAnna stares at the girls in their make-shift beds, sleeping in their new camp nightgowns from the store. The clothes they wore to the bonfire are in little folded piles at their feet.

"I hope this doesn't send them home with bad camp memories. There's nothing worse than that," JoAnna says.

"It's amazing how resilient children are. They seem to have taken it in stride. At least they weren't in the cabin when the fire started."

JoAnna says, "I'm glad no one was hurt. If someone wanted to harm the girls, they would have set the fire when they were in it. It's like someone only wanted to destroy the cabin."

"What makes you suspect someone did it deliberately? Did you see or hear anything tonight?"

"Oh, no. I just assumed. I mean how could a fire start on its own?"

"I'm sure the firemen will tell us all that tomorrow. Do you want some hot chocolate to help you sleep? There's probably some left."

"No, I won't have any trouble sleeping tonight."

After she walks out the door, I wonder what she meant by that comment. Did the excitement of the fire wear her out? There's something strange about her, but I can't quite put my finger on it. And she always seems to be sneaking up on me somewhere.

Purdue University 1995
Dear Diary,

College dorm life reminds me too much of summer camp. So many years ago but living with a group of girls again, I keep remembering Good Acres, the cabin, the snake, the wet sheets. Why can't I get those pictures out of my head? Maybe the only way to get rid of the pictures is to get rid of the girls who did this to me.

Mama's funeral last week made me realize that I didn't do enough to make her proud of me. But it's not too late. I'm going to get rid of those bad memories and once I'm free of them, I'll be the good girl Mama thought I was. Only the good girl. The one who is fearful and hateful will be gone.

Who Did It?

In spite of my makeshift bed, I must have slept hard the night of the fire because I don't remember tossing or turning, nor any dreams. When I wake the early morning sunlight is shining through the big Lodge windows. Jordan and the girls are still sleeping, their little bodies huddled together even closer as if they looked for comfort from each other in the night.

I tiptoe around them carefully. The big clock on the fireplace mantle says six. Way too early to wake them. Let them sleep as long as possible. As soon as they wake, they'll remember that they lost the new bathing suit in their favorite color or the potholder they made for their mother in crafts. The cooks will be banging around in the kitchen by seven to prepare breakfast and that will be the end of sleep for everyone.

I go to my cabin, shower and am grateful once again for Mari's little coffee pot which I set to brew. She's still sleeping, and I try to be quiet.

After breakfast, Paul gathers the Pottawatami girls in a circle on the porch and keeps them close to him so as parents come to claim them, he's able to explain what has happened personally.

He asks each parent to try to put a dollar value on what their child brought to camp, and he'll file a report with the insurance company. He jots their replies on his clip board and says he hopes he'll have checks for them as soon as possible. He says to each of them, "I'm so sorry for the lost articles money can't replace. The photos, their artwork, a favorite stuffed animal they brought from home to sleep with."

Most of the parents are thankful that no one was hurt.

One of the dads, however, makes a big fuss, and we feel sorry for his daughter, Stacey, as it obviously embarrasses her.

"Daddy, it's alright. Those clothes I had were getting too small for me anyway. Look, they gave us new tee-shirts, a sweatshirt, a cap and a new nightgown—all free."

"Well, that's the least they can do." He struts around the porch with his cell phone to his ear. We hope he isn't calling his lawyer.

Evidently no one answers his call. "I'll be getting back to you first thing Monday morning, young man," he says to Paul. "Let's go, Stacey."

The firemen return early in the morning and spend some time talking quietly to Paul while he sits with the girls waiting for parents.

Paul pulls me aside, "Kim, I need to meet with the staff briefly before they take their night off. I don't want anyone but you to know what the fireman told me. It appears to have been a deliberate fire, started in one corner of the cabin. There were signs of kerosene. I can't believe it. Who would do such a thing and why?"

"As far as we know everyone was at the campfire but Herb, Emma, the two cooks, JoAnna, and two sick campers, from Chippewa cabin." Who else might not have been there?"

"How about Pete and Shawn?" Paul asks. "Did you see them come down the tree after they sent the toilet roll? They could have returned to the cabins and no one would have noticed. We were all mesmerized by the fire and camp songs. We know they have access to kerosene."

Paul quickly makes a list of everyone on staff with a line beside their name.

"Kim, can you go to my office and make enough copies of this sheet for everyone?"

When I get back, he's addressing the staff. "First of all, I want to thank all of you for the great job you did last night, keeping the campers calm at the playground and up here at the Lodge. Courtney, the kids loved your Bear Hunt. So much so, that we might add that to our weekly schedule.

"Getting back to the fire. It was a shock to all of us but you handled it well. I'm so proud of you. The fire chief asked me to do one thing and it won't take long."

Then Paul looks down at his notes instead of the group. "They're not sure how the fire started."

I like that he can't tell a bold-faced lie to them eye to eye. That being dishonest is not an easy thing for him.

He goes on. "They're still working on it. We can't rule out anything. He asked me for a list of all people on the campgrounds last night and where they were at the time of the bonfire. I made a list of everyone on staff. Would you think for a moment of who you were sitting next to or who you can honestly say you saw at the bonfire for the entire time? Put a check beside their name. Put your name at the top of the sheet, please. It's very important. Only check those who sat next to you or who you actually saw. We need to account for everyone."

Seeing the confusion on several counselors' faces, he goes on. "I don't want to create suspicions and distrust among us, but the firemen are insisting on this list. If the fire wasn't an accident, if someone deliberately started it, well, that doesn't mean it was one of us. It could have been an outsider. That's the purpose of this exercise. To prove to the firemen that you were all with the group. I know in my heart none of you are capable of this. This way we can comply with his request and also clear our names."

He distributes the sheets. "I don't want in any way to destroy the family atmosphere we've created here the first two weeks. Let's take this negative incident and turn it into a positive by pulling our staff closer together. We can help each other get through this and come out stronger. I need your help, trust and cooperation more than ever."

I scan the area and see all eyes on Paul, and no one seems upset or resistant to his request.

"As soon as you fill out your form, you're free to go. Have a good Saturday night and we'll see you at noon tomorrow. If you have any questions or concerns, just come talk to me or call me. I'll be here all weekend."

Ever since Paul told me about the form, I've been thinking about who was sitting near me, so I make my checklist quickly and turn it in before most of the others. Not sure what to do then, but wanting to be of help if needed, I sit at a nearby table, out of the way but within earshot of Paul.

JoAnna walks up to Paul and says, "Do I have to fill this out since I wasn't at the bonfire?"

"Did you see anyone or anything after we left for the bonfire? Any noises? Anyone walking around?"

"I was sitting on my front stoop until dark and saw Emma walking to the lodge and getting into her grandfather's truck."

"What time was that?"

"I don't know. What time does it get dark these days? Maybe I went in a little before dark. It seems that's when the mosquitoes appear. Yes, just before dark."

"So you saw the fire after you went inside? And then you called 911. What time was that?"

"I don't remember, but the fire department can probably tell you. I'm sure they have a record."

"Were the flames high when you called?"

"Oh yes, it was going pretty strong before I noticed it. I smelled something burning and looked out the front door."

"Thanks, JoAnna. I'll tell the firemen what you said. They might want to talk to you themselves. Hope you don't mind going over it again if they do."

"Of course, I don't mind. We have to find the person who'd do such a terrible thing."

Hm. She doesn't know what the firemen told Paul. Wonder how she's so sure it was someone and not just an accident?

By now, most of the staff have completed their forms and are setting them on the table. Many of them take a minute to talk to Paul and assure him they will help in any way they can.

When Lucy comes up, she puts her paper on the stack beside Paul, then stands up on her toes to give him a big hug. It seems to me she hangs on for a long time and Paul makes no effort to let go.

Insecurity and jealousy are raising their ugly horns in me. Not now. Stay strong. What's that about Eleanor Roosevelt? Something about not giving consent. Yes, I'm not inferior. I'm as good as Lucy. As cute as Lucy. This is childish. Grow up.

Lucy is saying, "Paul, I'd be glad to stay here tonight if it would help. I hate for you to be alone after all this."

"Lucy, you're welcome to stay, but really, I'll be fine. Take your weekend break and come back fresh. Thanks anyway."

She replies, "I might leave for a little while. I need some things from home, but I wouldn't mind bringing some dinner back for you. How about it? What sounds good to you? How about I pick up a couple of steaks. Aren't there some grills down in the picnic area?"

"That's way too much trouble, Lucy."

"No trouble at all. I'll be back about seven."

Someone calls Paul's name and he walks toward the back of the Lodge while Lucy prances off.

I can't believe it. Is he agreeing to her suggestion? In the confusion, has he also forgotten about our Saturday night date? Our plans to go to the fish fry? I can understand his not wanting to leave the grounds with the fire investigation and all, but what about us? Doesn't he know I'll be staying here? Well, I'm not staying if he and Lucy are going to have a picnic—that's for sure. Anger burns in my gut. I spring up and storm to my cabin to pack an overnight bag.

Three's a Crowd

I get in my car and back out. Halfway down the driveway, I realize how childish it is not to tell Paul I'm leaving. Don't know yet if I'll tell him why because he seems to have forgotten about our plans. How unwise to care about someone again. To put my trust in them. Haven't I learned my lesson?

When I reach the bottom of the gravel road, I know I can't run off like a little kid. I make a U-turn in the entrance and return to the Lodge. By the time I get back, everyone is gone but Paul, who's putting a big paper clip on the stack of papers in his hand.

"Kim, there you are. Do you want to grab a bite of lunch and help me with these reports? We can tally them and see if anyone is missing."

He acts like I'm his buddy—his sidekick in crime solving. Sherlock and Watson. Cagney and Lacey. He has no clue that I'm hurting. Now I'm also frustrated because I'm dying to see the reports myself. I love puzzles and this is one I want to help Paul solve, but now I don't feel I can stay. He seems clueless as to what he has committed to do with Lucy. When is he going to tell me our dinner date is off? When Lucy shows up with two steaks? I'm not planning to be around for that Hallmark moment.

"Paul, I'm not staying tonight. I'd love to help you but I

need to leave now. I'll be here in time to open the store tomorrow."

A line furrows between his brows. "What's wrong? Is it the fire? Do you need to get away?"

Yeah, the fire in my heart. You put that out faster than a power hose. And then the words spill out before I think about them. A typical Aries move. "No, I don't need to get away, but it might be embarrassing for you when Lucy shows up with two steaks and there's three of us for dinner. We've put out enough fires for one weekend. That scene might be a little too hot to handle."

He looks confused. I rant on, "Or are you expecting me to wait in my cabin while you two have your picnic? Maybe you'll bring me a doggie-bag?" Sarcasm isn't my friend when I'm hurt.

"Oh, my gosh, Kim. There's been a terrible misunderstanding."

"Yes, on my part. I thought you were a decent guy, but it seems you're no different than the rest. A little blonde in short shorts bats her eyes at you and you can't say no."

The painful look on his face makes me feel I've been too harsh but I continue. "I know this has been a stressful time for you, Paul, and I don't expect to be wined and dined on Saturday night. I was perfectly willing to stay at camp and help you with those reports. Maybe get a clue as to what happened. But I can't believe what I overheard. And I wasn't snooping. I just happened to be beside you when—"

"When what?"

"When you agreed to her picnic."

"I didn't agree to anything. I told her not to bother."

"That's not what she heard. I'll bet my measly daily pay she shows up with those steaks thinking it's a dinner for two."

"Then I'm calling her right now. That's not what I want.

Believe me. Please, Kim, don't go."

There's sincerity in his eyes. I know how frightened he was over the fire. What a fool I am to cause him more grief. We aren't married or engaged. Just one dinner with him. I feel like a fool. As usual, I've spoken without thinking.

My anger dissolves into shame. "I'm so sorry. I have no right. You don't owe me your Saturday nights. I'm behaving like a spoiled child. You were right when you said I needed time. Guess I haven't healed over Mike and anytime I imagine I'm coming in second, I can't deal with it. I never used to be this way." Then to my further embarrassment, my own words cause me to tear up.

Paul's arms envelop me in a second. He holds me for a minute and then he cups my face in both his hands. "Please don't cry. I'm the one who's a fool. I was only half listening to Lucy. I've got so much on my mind. You are who I need now here with me. Help me get through this, please. This has nothing to do with dates or Saturday nights. I just need a friend now and I thought that was you."

I study his face and see the sincerity in his eyes. "It is me. I am your friend. I can't think of any place I'd rather be."

We hold each other tightly for another minute. It seems we've passed some unwritten boundary—not a sexual or passionate one. Our hug simply says we need each other.

I step back. There's still the Lucy thing.

"So, about those steaks, Paul. I'm telling you she's going to show up. You can't embarrass her or tell her not to come. She's on your staff and you have to work with her all summer. We have to find a way to make this acceptable—for her to save face."

"Maybe I should ask her to bring three steaks?" he asks with a guy's simple and stupid logic.

"No, trust me, that's not going to work. But you're on the right track. If we ask Lucy to bring four or five steaks—

if we have a group here, it would be easier for her to accept, rather than just me. We can help pay for them. Who else can we get to come back?"

"Maybe Herb? He's always here."

"No, that's not the answer."

"JoAnna was here last Saturday," Paul reminds me.

"You're right. We need to include her. That might just be the answer and make up for us leaving her alone last weekend."

"I'll call Lucy now. I need to find her application. Everyone listed their cell phones, I hope. Come to my cabin and we'll find it," he says.

As Paul digs through files, I say, "You should have that phone list handy, right above your desk. Why don't I, later this week, go through all their applications and compile a directory for you with their home and cell phones. Emergency contacts too." The fire has made me realize how we need to have those accessible.

"That's a great idea. Have I told you lately how glad I am that you're here?" His smile tugs at my heart. A few moments later, he glances up. "Good. Her cell number is on the list. Stay here with me a minute while I make this call, okay? I hope it comes out right." He punches in her number. "Lucy, good, I got a hold of you. It's Paul."

There's a pause and I can practically hear Lucy squealing on the other end.

"Yeah, that's the reason I'm calling. I found out several people are staying over tonight, and I hate to exclude them. You know, in light of what's happened, we should all eat together. I'll raid Edna's kitchen for some hamburgers for everybody. Would you mind?"

Lucy says something I can't hear.

"It's JoAnna and Kim and possibly Herb. And the maintenance boys might stay to help turn the art cabin into bunks."

Good thinking, Paul. Then I realize it's probably true. There's a lot of work to be done, and once again I was ashamed of my outburst.

Paul listens.

"No, no it's not a problem. I understand. In fact, it's a really good thing for you to take the night off. I'd leave myself except I told the firemen I'd be here all weekend—just in case."

Lucy says something else.

Paul responds, "I'll see you Sunday, and hey, thanks again for thinking of me."

When he hangs up, I ask, "What happened?"

"She said she forgot that her family was planning a get-together with some cousins who were passing through on their way to Chicago. In fact, she was just about to call me when I phoned."

Not likely. Lucy didn't have any plans until she heard she wouldn't be alone with Paul, but I keep silent. I've already said more than I should have at this point.

"Are the maintenance guys really staying?"

"I don't know if they'll spend the night, but they're going to work on that cabin this afternoon. Depends on how long it will take. Herb said he's taking them to Burger King for lunch and then they'll get started."

"We should be prepared to feed them tonight, just in case. Can we really raid Edna's freezer or should I buy some groceries?"

"Why don't you see what you can find in the kitchen? It shouldn't mess up the menu too bad to feed—let's see—eight people. But how about finding something for the two of us right now?"

"Sounds good. Then I can tally the staff's checklists if you need to be with the guys."

Paul puts the folder with the personnel applications back in his file but then asks, "Should I leave this out? I doubt you've got time to work on the directory now, but it's here when you need it." He places it on his desk.

"Good, maybe one night this week I'll get to that."

I go to the Lodge to scrounge up some lunch and find cold cuts, bread, and to my delight, huge canisters of my favorite hometown potato chips in the pantry. As I try to pry open the airtight lid, I understand why they always taste so crisp in spite of the humid summers.

After lunch, I walk to JoAnna's cabin. I didn't see her car in the parking lot, so I don't expect her to be there, but I leave a note on the door. If you're spending the night, join us for dinner—barbeque at the playground area about six. Kim.

Herb and the boys return, and to Paul's relief and surprise, Herb's truck bed is loaded with boxes of bunks. They drove to the new mall and found a Poplar Outfitters, the camper's paradise. The team seems proud of their purchase as they set one up. The beds are bright royal blue, a sturdy nylon fabric on steel supports.

Shawn, one of the heftier maintenance boys, stretches out on it to show it will hold his weight. "This is a lot nicer than what we have. I wouldn't mind having one of these myself," he says.

It doesn't take them long to move the arts-and-crafts tables out of the cabin, hose down the walls and floors and set up the cots. The only thing missing is the sign above the door. One of the boys volunteered to make one Sunday afternoon with the wood-burning tools we have in the craft room. We all agree it should be named Pottawatami II.

The boys are finished by five o'clock.

Paul says, "I can't thank you guys enough for staying late to finish this project. Herb, can you give them a day off in the middle of the week?"

"If we spread it out so they're not all gone on the same day, I can get by with the mowing."

"Good, I'll let you guys figure that out—and thanks again to all of you. Go on home now."

We haven't heard from JoAnna, so we don't heat up a barbecue grill or take any burgers out of the freezer. Instead, we go back to the Lodge and I show Paul the results of the tally sheets.

"I worked out a matrix and it looks like everyone is accounted for. You might want to check it yourself, but it seems everyone was at the bonfire—except the two cooks, Herb, JoAnna and the two sick campers. And little Emma."

"If this fire was deliberately started, it had to be an outsider. Herb locked the gate. He said he locks it every night about six, right after dinner."

"Someone could easily climb over the gate—it's not that high."

"I just don't understand. Why would anyone do this? And why that particular cabin? Thank God it didn't jump to the others. It easily could have, you know."

"Yes, I do know. Had it been one in the middle, it might have. I'm clueless, too, Paul."

Before we realize it, the time is seven and we haven't seen JoAnna.

Paul makes a circle on my arm. "This has been a crazy day. It might do us both good to get away for an hour or two. How about that fish fry? Can I cash in my rain check?"

"We'll have to leave a note for JoAnna in case she returns."

We go to our respective cabins to change clothes. This time I'm not so concerned about what I wear. This time I'm not trying to impress Paul. I'm just looking forward to an hour away from camp. I throw on some clean jeans and a lime green sleeveless shell. At the last minute, I grab my jean jacket but know I probably won't need it unless the air-conditioning in the restaurant is on high. But then again, a tall gin and tonic might take any chill off.

By the time we're ready to go, it's almost eight. Evidently JoAnna isn't planning on a barbecue so we head to her cabin. The note is still on the front door.

"Should I leave another note or just tear this one off?" Paul asks me.

"Let's leave it and add a PS."

8 PM. Since you weren't here, we left for a while. Be back soon. Kim. "At least she'll know we're thinking of her."

Summer, 2008

Dear Diary,

Revenge was challenging but easier than I thought it would be. After tracking Wendy down and stalking her for a few weeks, I discovered she was a hiker, so I hiked the same trail many times behind her and found a strategic spot to release the poisonous rattle snake. I wanted to do it at the top of the trail so it would take longer for help to arrive with an anti-venom. My research showed that if venom is not administered in thirty minutes, the bite could be fatal. It took several attempts and was getting rather expensive at $65.00 per snake. The first time the slimy critter slithered away into a bush instead of staying near the trail. I wasn't about to chase it. The second time didn't work either. If the trail plan didn't work I was going to figure out a way to put in her car while she was hiking. But the third time was a charm. Funny, I'm a snake charmer.

Once I released it, I turned around and started down the path. We passed each on the trail and I waited at the bottom, hoping for some sign of a scream. Finally, I did hear what sounded like a cry for help. I didn't know at that point if her scream was from an actual bite or just a scare. I was so tempted to run back just to enjoy the look of fear on her face, but I couldn't take the risk. She'd see me and wonder why I wasn't helping. I calmly waited, and when another hiker started up, I knew he would see her and call for help.

I was hoping for a longer time between hikers.

I returned to my car in the parking lot and waited to see what would happen. It wasn't long before I heard the siren of an ambulance. It pulled into the lot and two medics ran up the path with a stretcher. When they came back with her, I couldn't tell if the snake had done its job, but I watched the news that night and knew the mission had been successful. Hiker dies of poisonous snakebite on popular hiking trail.

The man at the nature center was right about the adult snake. I had always heard that the baby rattlers have the most deadly venom, but he said they don't often release enough to kill someone so I went with the adult snake.

Mama would have been proud of the way I handled this situation. She always said it pays to do your homework.

Twenty years of plotting and planning. Had I known how good it would feel, I would have done it sooner. I'll just bask in this good feeling for a while and plan my second move for next summer. The planning and anticipation is almost as good as the deed. Now I have something to look forward to each summer. Just like Mama always wanted.

Like Old Times

I retrieve my cell phone messages. "Kim, it's Lois. I talked to Trish Whipple. She'd love to get together. I haven't been able to reach anyone else, so why not the three of us for starters? Call me."

The following Wednesday Trish and Lois drive out to the camp in time to have dinner with one hundred campers.

The dining room is the usual bedlam. We join a table of staff members, Mari, JoAnna, Courtney and Lucy. I introduce them around and JoAnna's eyes seem to light up.

"JoAnna, you seem flushed. Do you feel okay?" I ask.

"Oh, I was out in the sun today helping put up the teepee. Maybe overdid it. But I feel good. Great actually."

"How'd you get rooked into that?" I ask. "Seems like a job for Herb's boys."

"It was actually my suggestion that we have a tent, so I felt I needed to pitch in."

"That's good, JoAnna. Pitch the tent?" Lucy is a quick wit. I hate it when cute girls also have a personality.

JoAnna continues. "I saw the tent in some of the old photos and asked Paul about it. You know how big he is on tradition. Wants everything to be the same as the years before."

"That's because big sisters tell little sisters how much fun they had, so we have to keep repeating everything for the newbies," Courtney adds.

"Well, it doesn't look to me like anything has changed at all," Lois says. "How's it looking to you, Trish?"

"The same. But smaller. The food's better than when we were campers. This is good stuff."

"Tell Edna. That will make her day," I say.

"So you girls were all counselors together? Is that the connection?" JoAnna asks.

"Yes, and actually one year, we were all in the same cabin as campers too. The Pottawatami Princesses." I add and the three of us laugh.

"Oh, yes, I'd forgotten that," JoAnna mumbles.

"Forgot what?" I ask.

"I read that somewhere in the photo album. That's what they used to call themselves. So what do you ladies do now?" JoAnna asks, seeming eager to change the subject.

Lois's mouth is full so I answer for her.

"Lois is a psychologist. Please, no jokes about needing one here at camp. Paul has already covered that. And Trish, I haven't had a chance to catch up with you myself. What are you doing these days?" I ask.

"Stay-at-home mom. I know that's rare, but I feel lucky that I can. My mom worked. I want it to be different for Betsy. She's five. I spend most of my day being her social chairman. She belongs to two playgroups. I myself don't have half as many friends to play with." She shrugs and turns to Kim. "You've found yourself a nice big playgroup here."

"You might call it that. It's been fun so far," I add.

Trish says, "I'd like to check in for a week. Not as staff; just a camper. Make moccasins, feather headdresses, lanyards, go swimming. Even that quiet time after lunch sounds appealing to me now."

"As if that hour was ever quiet in our cabin," Lois says. "What's on the schedule tonight?"

"Wednesday is free night. Nothing scheduled. Aren't they supposed to be practicing their skits for talent night tomorrow?" I peer at Courtney, the drama coach.

"Yep, tomorrow's the big show."

Trish says, "Oh my gosh, do you remember the year the lifeguards did the Motown skit? They were the Supremes or something. Miniskirts and wigs." I laugh and Lois joins in.

"Yes, and someone's wig fell off halfway through."

JoAnna says, "Oh that was a good one."

I glance at her. How would she know? She said she wasn't a camper.

When she turns toward me, she seems flustered and says, "I must be confusing it with something at the school where I work. They have a talent show each year, and they did the same thing." She swivels toward Trish. "So what do you ladies have planned after dinner? A walk down memory lane?" JoAnna is more talkative than usual.

"I'd like to sit on the front porch in those big chairs or on the swing we always raced for. Just watch the kids going up and down the hill," Trish answers.

"I'll spray you down with Off and see how long you last," I say. "The mosquitoes are the same as you remember too, and believe me, they're not smaller. Especially with all the rain we've had."

Lucy says, "Even if the kids are in their cabins, they'll make their nightly run to the canteen. Gosh, I covered for Billy last night and I couldn't believe the stuff they put away. They have huge appetites."

"And huge allowances. Inflation has caught up with Good Acres. And you thought we were protected from progress here in this secluded corner of the world," Mari says.

Trish tilts her head. "I thought that as I drove up the gravel road today. So close to two main highways, but once you get in those gates, the camp's like its own little planet, isn't it? You don't even know the rest of the world is out there. At least I never did."

"It always felt safe too. Protected. Maybe it was the woods surrounding us," Lois says.

"But doesn't Crazy Man Wilson live in the woods? How'd that urban tale ever begin anyway?" Courtney asks.

"It goes way back. Maybe Herb knows. The boys play it up more. I haven't heard the monster man mentioned all week," I say.

"Maybe he'll appear when the older girls get here. We don't want to scare the little ones. They're too sweet," Mari says.

"Let's not," JoAnna says. "I only have four cots in my cabin. Get them in a panic and I'll have more tummy aches than I know what to do with."

"Shall we adjourn to the outdoor parlor, ladies?" I ask. "Now one of the best perks of camp. Observe as I leave my dishes on the tray for someone else to wash. No cooking, no dishes."

"Sign me up," Lois says.

"Are you ladies going to visit us again?" JoAnna asks. "Maybe come to the closing bonfire ceremony one more time?"

Before they can answer, I say, "I should prepare you for something. Uh, we sort of had two bonfires last week. If you're looking for Pottawatami cabin, it's gone. Burned to the ground."

"What?" Lois's and Trish's eyes widen.

"We don't know how. Just a fluky thing. No one was hurt."

Lois says. "That's good. If the news gets out, Herb might as well lock the gate and throw away the key. No parent is going to send their kid to a camp after an incident like that".

"It was quite the blaze," JoAnna says. "Ironic, isn't it? Pottawatami means Fire Keepers." She stands as she speaks, takes her tray and leaves the table.

I almost tell Lois and Trish, "There's something not quite right about that one," but catch myself, not wanting to say it in front the other staffers.

Out of the Blue

The following Saturday, Paul and I decide to visit our parents in the afternoon and then meet in town for dinner before returning to camp for the night. The last camper is gone. We do our normal high-five and bask in the good feeling of another week done.

Just as we walk out the back door of the Lodge, another car pulls up the drive.

"Did we miss someone? Is there still a camper on the grounds?" Paul asks.

"Not that I know of. All the campers and counselors have left."

When the red Mustang convertible with its top down swings into a parking place, it's easy to see the driver. I gasp and grab Paul by the arm.

"Is that Mike? What's he doing here?" I ask.

Paul recognizes him too. "It sure looks like Mike. In person. Were you expecting him?"

"Expecting him? I stopped expecting anything from him months ago. Why would I expect him now? This is crazy."

Mike steps out of the car looking out of place in his dress pants and button-down shirt. City clothes. How does he even know I'm here? Of course, he knows the way to the campgrounds as we dated through college when I worked here, but what could he possibly want now?

"Mike, how are you?" Paul reaches for a handshake.

Mike shakes his hand, but it's obvious he doesn't recognize him.

"Paul. Paul Shrader. We went to high school together."

"Of course. How are you?" Mike responds.

I suspect Mike still doesn't have a clue and Paul knows it.

"It's been a while, hasn't it?" Paul says.

"About fifteen years." Mike answers.

I haven't said a word yet as I'm still in shock. Now Mike turns to me.

"Hi, Kim. Hope you don't mind my popping in like this. I was passing through, stopped at your parents' house and they said you were working here, so I thought I'd come by."

Thanks, Mom. Thanks a lot.

Paul says, "Listen, I'll run along. I'm sure you two have a lot to talk about." Without so much as a glimpse toward me, he walks toward his cabin.

"Paul, wait," I say, then realize I have to deal with Mike first. Deal as in get rid of him. "So, what is it, Mike? Good Acres isn't exactly on the way to anywhere. What really brings you here?"

"Can we go somewhere and talk? Can I take you to lunch?"

"I don't think so. I'm planning to have lunch with my parents. They're expecting me soon, so I don't have a lot of time."

"I see. Well, can we at least sit down somewhere for a minute?"

"We can sit on the porch."

We walk to the front of the Lodge and he heads toward the swing Paul and I always sit on.

"Let's sit here," I say pointing to two chairs. "That swing is too squeaky. Might drown out what's so important that you came all this way to say." My sarcasm is kicking in. Anger warning signs are flaring.

"You're looking great, Kim. The outdoors must be bringing out the best in you." Mike smiles as if that compliment can undo all the damage that has been done.

"I'm having a good summer. It's a nice change."

"Yeah, change. That's sort of what I want to talk to you about. I've been doing a lot of thinking and—" He stops and looks at me. I forgot how blue his eyes are. Light blue, like a perfect summer sky, I used to say.

"And what?"

"This is hard, but I think I made a huge mistake."

"What? You invested in the wrong stock?"

"Kim, don't. Don't be mad. Are you still that mad at me? Guess I can't blame you. I've been struggling with this for weeks now." He peers at the porch floor and then up at me. As handsome as ever in a Robert Redford way.

"If I came back, would you. . .would you give us another chance?"

I can't believe what I'm hearing. Mike admitting he made a mistake? That's the first shock. The second is that he thinks we can go back to the way we were. After his infidelity and his insensitivity to me through it all. I am so shocked I can't answer. Even my sarcastic mechanism has shut down.

Then I realize he might be mistaking my silence as a possibility that I am actually considering his proposal. Quick. I have to say something quick. I surprise myself when my answer isn't cruel. Mike seems pitiful, and I don't believe in hitting a man when he's down. "I'm sorry, but that's not an option for us anymore."

"Please, just give us a chance. Our good years of marriage. Doesn't that deserve a second chance? Doesn't it count for something?"

"It counts for what it was. Nothing more."

"But they were good years, weren't they, Kim? You have to admit. They were good."

"I thought so too once. But this past year has been hard for me. I've made a new life for myself and I can't go back now."

"What?" He scoffs. "You call this a new life? Working at a kids' camp. A job you had in college?"

His arrogant insult erases the pity I had for him a minute ago. In its place, a fury boils, rising like a witch's cauldron of dry ice at a Halloween party. "How dare you come here and belittle what I am doing. You can get in your fancy sports car and go back to 'your passing through' on the way to wherever you were going. I don't care to go with you or see you again. I'm sorry your life isn't working out, but it was your choice, not mine. And my choice now is not to see you again."

"I know you're angry. I know I hurt you. That's why I want a second chance to make it up to you. Don't you believe me?"

"Oh, I believe you. It must have taken a lot of courage for you to come here like this. But believing and trusting are two different things. I might believe you, but I could never trust you again."

"But it's over. You can trust me."

"This one might be over for you. But how do I know the next little cutie won't catch your eye? Or should I say fly?" I look at his crotch so there is no mistaking my intent.

He has the decency to blush.

"I've learned my lesson, Kim. I appreciate you more than ever. No one else can measure up to you."

"It's too bad you feel that way. Because I'm never coming back. I hope you can find someone who does measure up. Someone worthy of spending their life with you."

"Have you? Is that what this is all about? You've found someone else, haven't you? Is it that overgrown Boy Scout I just met? The one we went to high school with? Seriously, Kim, would his camp salary even pay the parking garage in your Chicago high rise? You can surely do better than that."

The distaste in my mouth rises, but I'm glad. It's making it easier to say the things I'd been wanting to for months. "Better? You want to talk about better? You'd better leave now before I say things you don't want to hear. Believe me. They've been bottled up a long time and it might not be pretty."

"Say them, Kim. Get them out of your system. Then maybe we have a chance."

"No more chances. No chance card. No passing Go. In fact, why don't you just go?" Why was I talking in Monopoly analogies at a time like this? I stand. "This conversation is over. My parents are expecting me."

"They won't mind if you're late. If you told them we're having lunch. You know, for old time's sake. I always liked your parents, Kim, and they like me. They seemed happy to see me today."

Had he always been so vain? Had I never seen it? Of course, my parents were polite. They're kind and courteous people. Too bad Amy wasn't there. She would have kicked his lying ass to the curb. But why hadn't they warned me that he was on the way?

"My parents did like you, but I doubt that they do now after the crappy way you handled the divorce. They're just too polite to be rude. And they don't even know the half of it."

"What do you mean?"

"I mean bringing your little concubine into our bedroom.

Couldn't you even spring for a motel room?"

He brushed that comment off with the wave of a hand. "I'm telling you it's over. Can't you forget it ever happened? Everyone makes mistakes. Nobody's perfect."

"I wasn't looking for perfect. I was just looking for a little fidelity. A little trust. I'm far from perfect either. But I'll tell you what. I'm perfectly fine without you in my life. Now would you please excuse me? I don't want to disappoint two people who do think I am perfect in every way."

I stride off the porch and leave him sitting in the knotty-pine chair. I hurry into my cabin to grab my purse and some clothes for dinner with Paul.

Paul.

I need to tell Paul that this thing—whatever it is—with Mike was out of the blue. I had nothing to do with it; nor do I want anything to do with it. When I come out of my cabin, Mike's sports car is gone. Unfortunately, so is Paul's.

Summer 2009

Dear Diary,

It's a good thing I perform only one revenge per year. It takes a lot of planning to commit the perfect crime. I had to stalk Sara for some time to find the right opportunity. She was a busy lady with those twins. Always carting them somewhere. I didn't think I'd ever get her alone.

I finally made friends with her in the park. The little girls made it easy. They were so cute that once I started praising her little darlings, Sara became putty in my hands. We forged a friendship of sorts as we sat on the bench watching the girls play on Wednesday afternoons. I had to borrow a friend's dog every Wednesday to have an excuse to be at the park.

Of course Sara never recognized me. Twenty years is a long time, especially when a girl goes from pre-teen to adult. Not to mention my new slim body and sassy hair color.

I probably earned her trust when I told her I had been a nanny all through college and now a private nurse for an elderly lady. Okay, so it was two little white lies. She said she wished she could afford a nanny. Just for a day. The opening I was looking for. When she said her birthday was coming up, I said, "Why don't you let me give you a birthday present? Take some time off. Go shopping, get a pedicure or something. I'll watch the girls."

Even though her pretty toes wouldn't show in her casket, it would be a nice way for her to go out with fancy red nail polish.

Ironically, the day I was babysitting, one of the twins wet her bed during her nap. How perfect. Sometimes things just fall into place and you know it was meant to be. I changed her crib and took the soiled sheet downstairs, waiting for Sara's return.

She came home almost giddy from her excursion. She couldn't thank me enough.

When she tried to pay me, I said I couldn't accept any money from her. She'd already given me so much.

She looked a little confused but probably assumed I meant the pleasure of watching the little girls.

"Yes, Sara, you've given me more than you realized through the years. Nightmares and anxiety and more hate than I thought I was capable of."

Now her confusion held a tinge of fright. But the look I was going for was humiliation. Like I had suffered.

"What are you talking about, Michelle?" I used a fake name from day one in case she told anyone about our park bench meetings.

"I'm talking about how you said you could smell pee-pee in the cabin. And you just had to tell the counselor so she checked all our beds. Then they hung my sheet out to dry so the whole camp knew what happened."

Sara still looked puzzled and now somewhat scared.

"Camp, Sara. Good Acres camp. Pottawatami cabin. The cabin that called me Pee-Pee Pat. All because of you. It's funny you've forgotten when I still remember it like it was yesterday. I wish I could have forgotten, but it plays over and over in my mind each day. I know how to make it go away though. Just like I made Wendy and the snake go away. The picture in my head of that snake died when Wendy did. Revenge is not only sweet. It's such a letting go.

Sara's eyes were showing terror. She started backing up, her mouth open as if she were trying to scream but nothing came out.

I took the crib sheet I had been holding behind my back and stuffed it in her face while I knocked her down and pinned her to the floor. My karate classes gave me such strength and so many ways to disable an opponent.

She tried to fight me, but I was strong. My years of anger gave me fuel—like a shot of adrenalin.

"How do you like the smell of that pee-pee? I was going to wet a sheet myself to remind you, but fortunately your little daughter did the job for me. I don't think I've wet the bed since camp. Well, a few times when I dreamed of what happened there, I had an accident or two. And each time I knew I had to rid myself of your memory."

As I talked, I took the long end of the sheet and started wrapping it tightly around her neck.

"If you have to pee, Sara, it's okay. In fact, if you would pee, I might let you go. We could say we were even. Go ahead, Sara."

As if she believed me, as if she thought she had a chance, a wet stain appeared on her light pink shorts. And then the look I was waiting for was there. Shame.

"Oh, Sara, that's a very bad girl. I can't stand the smell of pee-pee. I'll just have to punish you for that." I still had her pinned down, but then I tightened my grip around her throat. She kicked and kicked but when the kicking stopped, the job was done. Another camper avenged.

It was kind of me to leave the twins in their cribs so they wouldn't get hurt. After all, it wasn't their fault their mother had been such a mean girl. I knew their dad would be home in an hour. I made sure each twin had a bottle of water in their bed for when they woke up and I even turned on the music box, wearing my transparent latex gloves, of course, as I had the entire time I was there.

Free At Last

As I drive out of the campgrounds, I try Paul on his cell. No answer. I leave a message. "Paul, I'm driving to my parents. Sorry for the intrusion, the uninvited guest at camp. Can't wait to see you tonight. Please call."

When I reach the highway, I have to check my speed as I find myself flying. Such a sense of liberation fills me. I told Mike off. It feels great.

Now I know what Amy meant when she spoke of revenge. Although I didn't punch him out as she suggested, the verbal blows were good. They almost knocked him over, but the release I feel is even better. Had I known it would feel so good, I would have done it sooner. Just called him up and let him have it.

I wonder if that's how people feel when they physically hurt someone who has hurt them? I don't so much want to hurt Mike as I want to get rid of my own bad feelings. Maybe I had to hurt him as he did me to release them. Whatever. It worked. I'm feeling freer than I have for months—since before the divorce. Maybe even better. I'm taking charge of my life and it feels good.

I glance at my cell phone on the seat beside me as if I can will it to ring. When I flip it open, there's a message I haven't heard. At the next red light, I replay it.

"Kim, it's Mom. Just wanted to give you a heads-up that

Mike is on the way to camp to see you. It's about twelve-thirty now. Good luck. We'll see you this afternoon."

When I reach my parent's home, my mother greets me with a hug as if I'd returned from the Hundred Years' War. "Oh, Kim, I was so worried. I shouldn't have told Mike where you were. When I said you were working at camp, I had no idea he would head out there. What was I was thinking?"

"It's okay. Actually, I'm glad you did. I never would have agreed to meet him if he called, but just showing up that way gave me a chance to say some things that needed to be said a long time ago. I feel great."

I tell Mom what happened and also about my date tonight with Paul. She's beaming as I know she's hoping I can find someone to love again. Not any more than I am.

Although I leave my cell phone on all during my visit, it never rings. I find myself checking to make sure I haven't accidentally switched it to silent. The good feeling I have about telling Mike off is being replaced by a sense of dread that perhaps Paul is reading more into that visit. Why doesn't he call?

I leave one final message about five. "Hi, Paul. Just wanted to let you know I confirmed our reservation at Venice for 7:30. See you soon." We're trying out a new Italian restaurant one of the counselors raved about.

"Camp life must agree with you," my dad says as I come downstairs to say good-bye, dressed in a backless blue sundress that shows off my tan. In the sun every day, I need little makeup. Just a few touches of mascara and lipstick. Dad says, "You look beautiful."

"Oh, you probably say that to all the girls. Doesn't he, Mom?"

"Just the ones he loves," Mom says.

I suspect she'll be on the phone to Amy the minute I walk

out the door to tell her about Mike and Paul. I can't wait to tell Amy myself, but it's okay if Mom tells her. I don't want to deny her the pleasure.

Will He Show?

I'm so eager to see Paul I'm way too early. Also, because I'm not quite sure where I'm going, I leave myself time to get lost. Things have changed a lot since I left the area and some of the familiar landmarks are gone. Supposedly some new upscale shops near the restaurant and I'll check them out if I arrive too early.

I find the restaurant easily and do some window shopping, but my heart isn't in it. I want to see Paul. It's still only seven-ten, but I check my phone again to make sure I haven't missed any messages.

None.

I go into the restaurant, head for the bar and order my usual gin and tonic. As I sip it, I realize again how good it felt to say those things to Mike. It gives me such a sense of closure. As if I now have permission to move on in my life. To love someone again.

But my someone isn't here. Why hasn't he called me back? Did he read too much into Mike's visit? Surely, he wouldn't assume I was glad to see Mike.

Come on Paul, give me a chance to explain. My early euphoria is fading quickly with a sense of dread. Paul isn't returning my calls and that little voice of insecurity is getting louder by the minute. It's telling me Paul won't be at Venice.

At seven-twenty-five, my phone rings and the sound of

it almost knocks me off my stool. Is Paul calling? At last. Or perhaps to say he isn't coming.

It's Amy. "Is your date there yet?"

"No."

"Okay, just tell me when he comes, and we'll hang up. Mom told me about Mike. I'm so proud of you and just had to call. Way to go, girl."

"Thanks, Amy. It does feel good."

"You don't sound so good now. What's wrong?"

"I don't think Paul is going to show up. He got the wrong impression with Mike's visit."

"Oh, no. You need to tell him."

"Yes, I'd love to. But he hasn't returned my calls, and he's supposed to be here by now. Well, he's got two minutes before he's technically late."

"Okay, I'm getting off the phone. Call me later. I love you."

"I love you too." Just as I say those words, Paul is at my elbow.

"Who do you love? Are you talking to him again?"

"Oh, Paul." I throw my arms around him like a long-lost child. My hands remain on his shoulders when I pull away. "No, I'm not talking to him. That was my sister." I take a deep breath. "I am so glad to see you. Why didn't you call me back? I thought you were mad and not coming."

The gin has already gone to my head and my relief at seeing Paul and all the emotions of the day float to the surface. My eyelids smart. I blink back tears and look down.

He puts his hand under my chin and lifts my face close to his. "Hey, it's okay. Come on, let's get out of this place for a minute."

Paul helps me hop off the stool and takes my arm as we walk past the reservation desk. He nods to the hostess as we walk out. "We have a seven-thirty reservation but could you hold our table a few minutes, please."

Outside, we walk past people waiting for a table to a bench on the sidewalk.

Once we're alone, I turn to him and kiss him on the lips. Then I say, "Does that answer your question?"

"What question?" He kisses me back.

When I come up for air, I say, "You asked me who I love. It certainly isn't Mike. I didn't know he was coming. I didn't spend ten minutes with him. Only long enough to tell him I never want to see him again. And when I left, you were gone."

"I'm sorry. I had to get out of there. I imagined all sorts of scenarios. That he wanted you back. That it was what you wanted. I felt like that nerdy kid in high school again. On the sidelines."

I pull him closer to me again. "I'd say now you're on the goal line. In fact, you're about to score a touchdown right here."

"Really, I'm going to score? Right here on the sidewalk?" He laughs.

I laugh too and we hug each other as if we've been apart for years. "Let's get our table and I'll tell you all about it."

If the counselors who recommended the restaurant would later ask me if the food was as good as they said, I couldn't tell them. I do remember eating some sort of delicious pasta, but mostly I remember Paul's warm brown eyes across the candlelit table. A little table for two in a back corner. When the violin player comes to our corner to play, Paul's hand covers mine and my heart is singing the words, That's Amore.

I know I'm sinking, falling into the love pit and doing what I said I would never do again. But surely Paul is someone I can trust, isn't he?

An Ariel View

If one flew over Good Acres with tonight's translucent and all-knowing sky view, one might see the following after hearing revelry over the loudspeaker at eight-thirty.

Emma in bed at Grandpa's house, nose in her latest Nancy Drew. Herb in the rocking chair on his front porch smoking a cigar that is his one guilty pleasure when the day is over. Jordan and Jesse in the third-floor lounge sitting side by side on a worn-out lumpy sofa holding hands and promising to write to each other from their respective colleges in the fall. Edna propped up against her pillows in bed in her yellow chenille robe, curlers in hair, her nose in a Diane Mott Davidson culinary mystery, Dying for Chocolate. She's considering trying one of the recipes in the back of the book and wonders if Herb loves chocolate. Mabel reading her Bible and choosing her scripture for tomorrow. She highlights Proverbs 24:3. Above all else guard your heart for everything you do flows from it.

Mari quietly swimming laps in the pool with just the side lights on, her alone time with not a camper in sight. She silently glides from one end to the other with barely a ripple, gracefully making the turn of an expert swimmer The maintenance boys in the basement of the Lodge having their nightly competitive game of Foosball. The girls in the Iroquois cabin digging into a box of homemade cookies one of the mothers sent and discussing the merits of peanut butter vs. chocolate chips.

Paul and Kim on the front porch swing where he plays with the curly tendril that's fallen out of her ponytail. Her eyes are closed but she's smiling, like she's just heard a private joke.

An occasional scent of fresh-cut grass wafts through the night air, mixed with the scent of a flowering bush near the front porch. Away from city lights, the stars are bright in a moonless night.

The porch light is on at the nurse's cabin for middle-of-the night tummy aches who might seek her out. Inside JoAnna, still in her scrubs, sits at her desk and writes in her nightly journal. One would assume it's a record of medicine dispensed at camp today, but if one could zoom in closer, one would see it's not a journal but a diary. A private diary.

Face in the Window

We are now in the fourth week of camp for the girls. This week it's girls, ages eleven to twelve. Little Emma is no longer an official camper as there is too much age difference, but I see her occasionally at meals when she visits her grandfather.

During the hour after lunch when all the campers return to their cabins for "quiet time," I find Emma sitting on the front porch of the Lodge. Emma and Nancy Drew.

"Hi, Emma. Have you solved the latest mystery?"

She holds up her book, The Secret of Shadow Ranch. "Not yet."

"You're such a good detective. Maybe you can help us solve the mystery of how the fire started in the Pottawatami cabin. Did the fire chief ever ask you any questions about that night?"

"Yes, he asked me if I saw or heard anything unusual while I was reading in the cabin?"

"Did you?"

She places her bookmark carefully in its place, closes her book and squeezes her eyes tight as if she is trying to remember. "No, there was nothing unusual. But it was kind of scary for a minute because that was the night I was reading The Secret of the Old Staircase. Do you remember that one?"

"No, I don't think so."

"Well, it's about a ghost in this old house. It's Nancy's friend's grandmother's house. The ghost makes strange noises all the time. And every time Nancy hears the noise, she runs to the room, but there's no one there. She knows there's a secret passage but she can't find it. And then one night, Nancy sees a scary face in the window. And that scared me because that's just when I thought I saw a face in the cabin window."

"You saw a face? Who was it?"

"It was just Nurse JoAnna."

"JoAnna? What was she looking for?"

"I don't know because I didn't talk to her. I didn't know it was her at first. When I got up to look, she was already walking away. I don't think she saw me get up."

"You were brave to walk to a scary window."

"I wasn't going to. But then I wondered if it was my imagination because of the ghost story, you know. So I crawled to the window on the floor just like Nancy did and then I peeked out. And that's when I saw JoAnna walking back to her cabin."

"What did you do then?"

"I finished the last three pages of that chapter and went to the Lodge to meet Grandpa. He was waiting there in his truck."

"Did you tell any of this to the fire chief?"

"Don't think so. Because he asked me if I saw anything unusual. Seeing Nurse JoAnna isn't unusual. It's not like she's a stranger at camp or anything like that."

Summer 2010

Dear Dairy,

I wasn't really planning on the fire, but then I thought, why not? I was tired of looking at that cabin that housed my bad memories. What rotten luck that it was on the end where I could see it each day and relive all the bad things that happened to me there. Why not just get rid of it? A fitting end for its name—Keeper of the Fire.

I thought of this as a little bonus revenge since the main revenge is still due this month. One a year. It's possible that with this last one, I'll be done. And getting rid of Pottawatami forever should cinch it. I didn't want to hurt any of this year's campers. It wasn't their fault. I thought that little bookworm, Emma, was going to mess things up really good. The first time I looked in the window to plant the kerosene paper roll, I saw her reading on her bed. She wasn't supposed to be there. I went back to my stoop to think about how to get her out of there without her suspecting anything, and then a few minutes later she walked out the door and up to the Lodge where Herb's truck was parked.

As soon as they rode back down the road to his house, I checked on my two patients. They weren't asleep but lying quietly on twin beds across from each other just talking. I gave them each a half of a Popsicle and said, "I'll be out on the porch stoop if you need anything, girls."

When I saw and heard how the boys lit the bonfire last weekend, I thought what a clever idea. So I doused a toilet-paper roll of my own in kerosene, hid the can in the trunk of my car until I could get rid of it and dropped the drenched roll into the back cabin window. Then I took a long wooden match—the kind you use for fireplace lighting. I lit it and threw it through the open back window like a dart, trying to hit the toilet paper roll. I had been practicing that shot a lot, and darn if I didn't get it close enough to ignite.

Then I went back to my stoop to watch the bonfire. Maybe they were singing camp songs at the bonfire, but I doubt they had as much fun as I did watching my bad memories go up in flames. Once it got going, I went inside and called 911 like a concerned citizen should. Mama always said we had a civic duty. I checked on my two patients and they were still talking quietly with purple lips from their Popsicles. I wanted to be a good nurse because I never forgot how nice the camp nurse had been to me.

I'm looking forward to the good night's sleep I always have after my revenge deeds.

A cleansing, so to speak.

What's in a Name?

I try to remember to check phone messages on my Chicago phone landline every couple of days but I have few calls as my editors now use my cell phone. I'm not expecting anything exciting and I'm right. The dentist office called saying I'm overdue on my six-month checkup. I call them to reschedule but I keep getting a fast busy on my cell, so I resort to Paul's office landline.

The stack of personnel folders we pulled out last week sit on the desk, and I remember the phone directory I said I would make for Paul. After my call to the dentist, I take them into my cabin and sit at my laptop. Some twenty names. Won't take long.

I make a spreadsheet with four columns. Name, Home Number, Cell Number, Comments. The applications are in alphabetical order and phone numbers are easy to find at the top of the first page. Some of the apps have credentials clipped to them, as well as their reference letters. Mari's application has her Red Cross Swimming Instructor certificates. One for Michigan, one for Indiana. Lucy has a copy of her Indiana teaching certificate attached. I'm tempted to peek at her references, but know I shouldn't be ruffling through confidential papers.

I'm almost done with the list when I get up to use the bathroom and manage to knock the folder on the floor, scattering papers everywhere. Great. I shuffle the papers back in order. Most of them still have paper clips but some have come loose. It doesn't take long to match loose papers with applications, but I end up with one transcript with a name I don't recognize. Patricia Jo Mann.

I look at the school and year the degree was confirmed. Bachelors in Nursing, Purdue University, 1998. I find JoAnna's application. Under education, it lists Purdue. A degree in nursing. There are also several reference letters attached. One is from an elementary school. The letterhead says Portage School District. A glowing reference of her organizational skills and JoAnna is especially sensitive to the children's needs. She is a welcome member of our staff. Signed by the principal, Luann Branch.

Evidently Patricia Jo Mann and JoAnna Parsons are the same. Interesting. Lots of people use their middle name, but she never mentioned being married. I wonder if she still is.

Scrubs and Burgers

It's the fifth and last week of camp for girls ages twelve and thirteen. Now we are beginning to get repeat campers—those who have been here previous summers, and we can tell the difference. As they arrive on Sunday and the Lodge begins to fill, old friends greet each other. Most of them are familiar with the rules and routines. Some are sad to see Pottawatami cabin gone, but we try to make the new location special.

"Look how close we are to the Lodge and pool." Jordan tells one of them.

I wink at her as I pass. "Nice sales job."

Although I'm busy with my Sunday sweatshirt sales, I can keep an eye on the activities in the main Lodge through the open double doors. The instructors are on hand although they don't have much to do but mingle with the parents. Lucy is shadowing Paul, as usual. The girl's persistent. I have to give her that.

Between sales and chatting with the parents, I am basking in the glow of my time with Paul and our usual Saturday date night. After dinner, we returned to the campgrounds and ended up on the porch swing as we always do. Had he pursued it, I would have happily gone to his cabin, but for now, spoonin' on the squeaky swing, as he calls it, is just right.

Watching him laugh with Lucy now, that twinge of the old insecurity returns, and I give myself the pep talk. Okay, I'm not inferior. Don't consent to it. I turned the corner with Mike issues. Don't let insecurity creep back in. Paul isn't Mike. He can be trusted. Believe in myself.

"How much are the hooded sweatshirts?" One of the parents asks, bringing me back to reality.

After the first rush of campers who waited at the gate to enter, the flow trickles in steadily, but we aren't overwhelmed.

"How's it going?" JoAnna asks as she peeks into the store.

"Good. It's amazing what a few degrees of cooler weather can do for sweatshirt sales."

"I'd love to help you. It looks like fun, but I have to man my station. You wouldn't believe how many prescriptions these kids are now bringing to camp."

In my days as a camper and counselor, I never saw the nurse wear a white uniform as JoAnna does on Sundays. It's a nice professional touch. "I like that you wear your uniform on Sundays. It reassures the parents."

"I think so too. Although the kids are surprised when they see me later in the week in a camp tee-shirt."

"I like when you wear scrubs—I bet those are really comfortable."

"They are. You know there's a store with nothing but scrubs at the outlet mall?"

"Really? The whole store?"

"Yes, would you like to run over some afternoon with me? I can get away for a few hours. I could use a few more."

"Sure, that would be great. Let's do it."

JoAnna and I drive to the mall Tuesday during the dinner hour, thinking that's when we'd be missed the least and can get a bite while we're out. I'm curious to find out if she has been married, but I don't want her to know I was in the personnel files. Surely there's some kind of rule against that.

"So tell me, JoAnna, have you ever been married? You're so good with the girls I know you'd make a great parent."

"I was married for a few years. We never had kids. Probably for the best since it didn't work out."

"Yeah, me too. It's hard enough being single, but being a single parent would be even harder."

"Oh, I didn't know you had married."

"Yes, almost ten years. He was a few years behind in the seven-year itch. But it came anyway. I'm finally getting over it. I've gone back to my maiden name since we didn't have children." I don't add that it's also because I don't want any reminders of Mike. "This summer has helped a lot. Restoring my confidence, you know."

"I never would have imagined you would have a confidence issue. You always seemed so sure of yourself."

Did she say seemed or seem? Always seemed so sure of yourself sounds like she knew me before. "Didn't you tell me you never went to Good Acres?"

"That's right, I didn't."

"It's just that you seem so familiar with everything, like you've been here before."

"I have a cousin who was a camper here and I remember coming to pick her up with her parents one Saturday. Always wished I could come."

"So, do you have some time off? Between camp and the start of school? Do you like to travel?"

"No plans this year. I've always wanted to take a long cruise. Maybe next summer."

"Oh, not planning to return?"

"I doubt it. My time here is done. It's been good, but time

to move on. How about you? Will you be returning?"

"I haven't even thought that far ahead. It's been a nice change for me, but I doubt I'll return. Maybe by then I'll have a real job. Hard to say."

We go to the scrub store and I help JoAnna pick out a few outfits the kids might like. One has little bears all over it and the other has cars and rockets for when the little boys come.

We stop at a Sonic Drive-in between the mall and the campgrounds.

I say, "You know, sometimes there's nothing as good as a greasy burger and fries, is there? I should be really bad and go ahead and have the chocolate milk shake too."

JoAnna comments, "I have to be so careful. You know I used to be quite heavy."

"Oh really? You'd never know it. You're quite trim. How did you lose the weight?"

"I lost it in nurses training when I was made aware of how important good nutrition was. Also got away from my mom's cooking. Actually, it was probably more her nagging about my eating habits that caused me to eat more instead of less."

I nod. "Funny how that works, huh? I just lost thirty pounds I packed on after the divorce. Some nights I sat down with a tub—not a dish, mind you, but a whole tub—of ice cream. I read somewhere that Jen did that when Brad left. The only difference is she probably did it once. I made it a nightly ritual."

"Did it make you feel better?"

"Of course not. Worse. I was still lonely and depressed, and now I was fat, lonely and depressed."

JoAnna laughs. "You're so funny, Kim. I always wished I could be more like you."

"Always? You just met me."

"I meant I wished I could be more like girls like you while I was growing up. Cute, funny, lots of friends."

I feel sorry for JoAnna. "I don't think you have any problem making friends. In fact, why don't you join us this weekend? Some of the girls who were counselors are spending the night Saturday. You met them at dinner last week. How about it?"

"Really? They wouldn't mind?"

"I don't see why not. We had hoped to have a bigger group but can't find all of them. Not to mention some have already died."

"That's strange."

"Yeah, tell me about it."

"Well, I'd love to join you. Will you be staying in one of the cabins?"

"That would be fun except our cabin was Pottawatami. The new one won't feel the same."

"We'll have the tent up by then. Why don't we all sleep in the tent?"

"Hey, that might be fun. I'll ask them."

We are almost back to the turnoff for camp when JoAnna says, "Look up ahead. Is that a roadside garden stand? Could we stop?"

"Sure." I slow down to pull up to the stand.

JoAnna jumps out and appears excited. She walks around eyeing all the flowers displayed.

"Looking for anything special?" A lady in a gardener's apron approaches us.

JoAnna says, "Do you by chance have any foxglove?"

The gardener says, "Actually, I do. I have some lovely yellow and pink." She leads us to a table around the corner. "Do you have a preference?"

JoAnna studies the plants carefully. "Oh, the color's not important."

"Really? Most people shop by color."

"Well, sure," JoAnna says quickly. "I'll take some of each color. In fact, I'll take all of these."

"All of them? Must be a big party," the gardener says and gathers them in her arms.

JoAnna carries a handful and I pitch in also, carrying them to the makeshift checkout table.

Back in the car I say, "JoAnna, what in the world?"

She appears pleased with herself. "A little surprise. You'll find out later."

By the time we return, the girls are running relays on the front lawn. Two campers are sitting on the nurse's cabin stoop waiting for their evening meds, and it's time to open the canteen for bedtime snacks. Or dentist's job security, as I call it. The kids' nightly sugar fix.

"Thanks for going with me," JoAnna calls over her shoulder. "I can't wait for the girls' weekend."

I walk away hoping the others won't mind. The gleam in JoAnna's eye makes me feel I did the right thing to include her.

Summer 2010

Dear Diary,

I can't believe how fate is playing out my hand—bringing Trish right to me. It's almost too easy. Lois and Kim were never that mean, but they did go along with the others, so in a sense they were just as guilty. Maybe I can do a three-in-one and put an end to this matter once and for all. Wasn't it Trish who said my shorts were big enough for a tent? We'll see how she feels about tents before this summer is over. Maybe not so big as tight. Cutting-off-the-circulation tight. Or perhaps one of those spears that hold the tent down. That could do some serious damage.

Mama always said to be resourceful. I'm trying to use what materials are at hand. And that roadside stand sold flowers. A stroke of luck there.

I don't know when camp has been as much fun as it has this year. The prospect of taking three of them down at once. What a finale. Yes, planning is half the fun. I remember how Mama used to plan her dinner parties with long lists of things to do. She taught me so many valuable skills. She would be happy to know I'm using them for a good cause. To rid the world of hurtful people

Once I pull this off, I probably won't come back. What's the point? It will be done. Complete. I'll spend my summers vacationing in places with much better accommodations than this. That Mediterranean cruise brochure looks lovely.

A Quick Kiss

I pop into Paul's office. "Paul, if you can spare me one night this week, I'd like to go have dinner with my friend, Lois. The one you met. She wants me to meet her husband and kids."

"No problem. There is a curfew though. Gate closes at ten."

"Ten? I thought Herb locked it at six."

"He does. I just meant for you. You'll turn into a pumpkin or something if you come home later." He slips his arms around me. "I just want to know you're home safe in your bunk. In your little cabin right behind mine."

"Wouldn't it be safer if I was in your cabin?"

"Oh, no. That wouldn't be safe at all. Not for either one of us."

He kisses me and I know I'm not safe around him anymore.

"Hey, what if a camper walks in? News of this kiss would spread like wildfire through the camp."

"You've got that right. Gosh, I hope I don't have the microphone for the PA system on."

"Paul!"

"Just kidding. Come here."

He grabs my arm and opens the accordion door that separates the office from his living quarters. "Have I ever given you the personal tour?"

"Well, not exactly."

He leads me through his living area into his bedroom and points to the window. "I can see your cabin from here every night. Even know what time you turn your light off."

"Aren't you the creepy big brother?" I laugh.

"It's my job. Just taking care of my staff." He wraps his arms around me again, and his kiss leaves me weak in the knees. His bed looks inviting. "I'd love to take care of you, Kim."

"Isn't it nap time for the campers or something?" I ask.

"I wish. We'd better get out of here before we're both reported MIA."

"Yeah. Big emergency. Someone dropped a lanyard stitch. I really must go."

As I leave his office, Herb is walking in. Close call. Almost caught in the director's private quarters. The sheepish smile Herb gives me tells me we've been caught anyway.

Lies

"How would you like to play Camp Director for one night?" Paul asks en route to my cabin after lunch.

"Uh, me thinks there is a catch here," I raise one eyebrow in his direction.

"No catch," he says with a little laugh. "Just a favor. My sister invited me to dinner. It's been a while since I've seen my nephews."

"Family time? Of course. I'm all for it. Reporting to duty." I give him a mock salute.

"You know the routine. Announce over the PA that the canteen is open from seven to eight. Play taps at eight-thirty. Stay in my cabin till I get back so you're available for any concerns. Answer the phone."

"I can handle that, "I say.

"Oh, there is one more thing." He turns and cups my chin in his hand. "Put on a sexy camp tee-shirt and be waiting in my waterbed."

I burst out laughing. The camp tee-shirts are about sexy as a pair of granny bloomers, and there's no way we would ever attempt anything so risky on the campgrounds.

I wave good-bye to Paul as he pulls out of the parking lot just before dinner. Later, after playing taps from his cabin's sound system, the office landline rings.

"Director's cabin," I answer. "This is Kim."

"Is Paul there?" A woman's voice asks.

"No, he's not here this evening. Can I take a message?"

"It's his sister, Maggie. We wanted to set up a time when he could have dinner with us. The boys were asking about him."

"But, isn't he—?" I start to reply and then think better of it. "Would you like him to call you?"

"That would be great. Thanks."

I try to ignore the sick feeling in the pit of my stomach. Didn't he tell me he was having dinner with the nephews tonight? It's dark when I walk back to my cabin. I'd been looking forward to Paul's return this evening, hoping he wouldn't be too late. My plan was to do some editing of the piece I had written earlier today and then wait on the porch swing for his car to come up the crunchy gravel driveway. Maybe we could have some spoonin' swing time, as he calls it.

"What a low-down liar," I say to myself. "And the nerve to ask me to wait in his waterbed, even as a joke. Why? So he could whisper some sweet-nothing lies to me? Nothing but lies." I storm into my cabin and am glad that Mari isn't there. Angry and confused and I don't want to talk about it.

I open my laptop but can't focus on what I'm reading so I slam it back down and head to the Lodge. The kitchen is dark when I enter by the back door. Some of the counselors are sitting around one of the tables in the main dining room and they have an IPOD playing music. No one sees me, or if they do, they don't pay any attention.

I switch on a light in the pantry, which isn't visible in the Lodge, find the big can of potato chips and stuff my face as I stand there in the pantry. Handful after handful until I'm going to be sick on the grease, but it seems like no matter how much I stuff in my mouth, it doesn't fill the empty space inside since I hung up the phone.

A car pulls up in the driveway. I turn off the light and wipe my face with the bottom of my tee-shirt, knowing there are probably greasy crumbs stuck to my lips and chin. At the landing of the stairway, I look out the window of the door leading to the parking lot. Lucy's getting out of her car. Alone. As she walks to her cabin, another car pulls up. It's Paul's. He jumps out of his car, calling out.

"Hey, Lucy, you know there's a curfew, don't you?"

"I beat you home, didn't I?"

They both laugh, and my heart sinks.

When Lucy's in her cabin, I leave the Lodge and see Paul gathering some books out of his back seat. "So how was dinner with your nephews?" I call out.

He turns quickly. "Hey, Kim, you scared me there in the dark. I was hoping you'd still be up. Give me a minute here and we'll sit on the porch."

"Sure, I'd love to swing on the porch." Can't wait to swing with a swinger like you.

"Be there as soon as I drop off these books."

I head to the front porch and see the counselors leaving for their respective cabins.

Paul runs up the stairs like he's on steroids. What a slime ball. Lying and sneaking around, and he doesn't even have the decency to be ashamed. Bouncy like a kid out of class.

I want to confront him immediately but wonder how long he'll keep the farce going. "So, how are the little nephews?"

"Fine, just fine. How about you? What did you do tonight? I missed you." He sits beside me and puts his arm around my shoulders.

It's that last piece of lying crap that causes me to blow. "Oh, you missed me? That's funny."

"What? Didn't you miss me?"

"Well, it seems someone else is missing you. Your sister called and said the boys really would like to see you. She wanted to set up a time for you to come to dinner."

Even by the dim porch light I can see Paul's face turn ashen. "Oh man." He closes his eyes and shakes his head. "I can't believe it."

"I'd like not to believe it myself. But first her call and then I see you and Lucy arriving home within minutes. Some planning to take separate cars."

"What are you talking about?"

"Well, isn't that what you were doing? Why else would you lie to me?"

"You've got it all wrong."

"Yeah, I'm wrong for sure. Wrong thinking I could trust someone again. I really thought you were different."

"Kim, you can trust me."

"Oh sure. Sorry, but this scenario is a little too déjà vu. Hope you can find a craft person for the boys' session. I can't imagine spending another five weeks here with you."

"I'm sorry I didn't tell you the truth, but I was planning to tell you eventually."

"Oh really? And when? When you and Miss Archery got engaged? What were you waiting for?"

"Listen to me. I don't know where Lucy was tonight, but she wasn't with me. I had—"

"Had what?" I don't wait for him to finish. I bolt from the swing and run off the porch. Instead of going to my cabin, I head for the craft cabin. I don't want to explain anything to Mari. I need to be alone.

I go in and pull on a cord that lights the single 100-watt bulb. The cabin isn't designed for evening use. During the day, the side panels open to let in the natural light. There among paper, crayons, paint and glue, I sit on a bench of one of the picnic tables and wonder why I have been so gullible.

Barely a minute passes when the door of the cabin creaks open and Paul walks in. He stands in front of me, takes a deep breath and seems to square his shoulders. "Kim, what I had to do was go to a meeting. An AA meeting. I'm a recovering alcoholic." His eyes seem to be pleading for understanding, or is it for acceptance?

I'm too dumbfounded to speak. I start to say, "Paul—"

He blurts, "I was going to tell you. Really I was. So many times, I wanted to but it never seemed the right time. No one here knows, and I don't want to lose this job. I love it here."

I still don't know quite how to respond. My feelings are a jumble. Relief that he has not lied, shame that I suspected him of wrongdoing so quickly, and

admiration for his honesty. A strong urge overcomes me to reach out and hug him, but I hold back. Finally, I simply ask, "How long?

"Six years now. At first I went to meetings weekly, then gradually monthly. Now just occasionally." He goes on, "I didn't see the need to tell you at first, but the more I've come to care for you, the more you need to know this about me. Honest, I wouldn't have kept it from you. Do you believe me?"

I stare into his brown eyes, pleading eyes. "Yes, I do believe you. I'm sorry for what I thought."

"Don't be sorry. You had every right. I was wrong not to tell you sooner."

"Did something prompt you to go now?" I recall the times we've eaten out and I'd order a gin and tonic. Was I a bad influence? And why didn't I notice that he was not drinking alcohol? I recall now that once he said he took his designated-driver role seriously, and once he said he just needed something carbonated. I never gave it much thought.

"You've heard, I'm sure, of the twelve-step program. I've been through all the steps in the past six years, but last week I slipped a little."

"You had a drink?"

"No, just a little setback. I could tell you about it if you—"

In spite of wanting to give him my full support at this time, I feel so drained. "I would like to hear about it, but I'm so tired right now. I wouldn't be a very good listener."

He says, "I hope this doesn't change anything between us. I'm sorry you had to find out this way."

"I accept your apology and I appreciate your confiding in me now. We do need to talk more about this, but right now I'd just like to sleep. I'm really wiped out."

"Sure, I understand," he says. "We'll talk later." He reaches up and pulls the light cord and takes my hand to lead me out of the now darkened cabin. At my place he simply gives me a hug with no attempt of a good-night kiss. Once again he says, "I'm sorry."

Mari is in bed reading when I enter. "Hey," she says without looking up.

"Hey, yourself," I say. "I'm going to sit out for a while. Beautiful night." I nab a bottle of water and sit on the front stoop. Paul's bedroom light is on, and I almost walk to his cabin to see if he wants to talk. I feel bad for not letting him express himself further. But I stay on my stoop alone with my thoughts, all in a jumble. For some reason, I'm confused even though Paul's explanation should have relieved any anxiety I had.

My positive self-talk says something like, "Forget it. Move on. Paul can be trusted. He's not Mike." The other voice, the one I've come to dislike, says, "You'll never be able to trust anyone again. One little slipup and immediately you think they're cheating. You think you're the victim."

Wonder if there's a 12-step program for people like me.

Good-Bye Girls

Paul and I don't have time to talk on Friday, a busy day for the girls. After the bonfire is extinguished and the campers are in bed, we have a little going-away party in the Lodge for the counselors as it's their last week. Ten male counselors will arrive tomorrow afternoon for their orientation with Paul. On Sunday the first boys, ages seven and eight, arrive.

Saturday morning Paul and I watch the last car pull out of the driveway about one in the afternoon. As has become our ritual, we turn and high-five each other.

"Whew, another week with no casualties." He wraps his arms around me in his familiar hug.

Then he pulls away and puts his hand under my chin, tilting it upwards close to his face. "I hope you and I aren't a casualty after Thursday night. Can we talk now? We have—what?—five hours alone? Just the two of us."

I take both his hands in mine. "Not exactly five hours. You have some male counselors showing up in a few hours and my friends could be arriving as soon as three and—"

"Friends? You have friends? Besides me? Since when?"

"Since 1987, if you must know. Remember that Girl Scout song we sang at the campfire last night? I sing the little jingle. Make new friends, but keep the old. One is silver but the other is gold."

"So how do I move up to this gold status?" He tugs gently at the loose tendril of hair falling on my cheek.

"You could earn a gold star if you set up a little campfire for us tonight. My friends want to go to the clearing—one of their fondest memories."

"Do you want the fireball to come out of the sky? Not sure I can do that as well as the maintenance boys do."

"No. Absolutely no tree climbing and no kerosene-soaked toilet paper rolls. I've seen enough fire for one summer. It's sad we won't be able to sleep in our original Pottawatami cabin."

"I can move some of the logs so you can sit closer to the fire pit. How many of you will there be?"

"Just three of us. Not a very good percentage out of ten. Or should I say out of eight since two are dead. Still creeps me out." I give a little shiver. "Make that four. I invited JoAnna. She seems so lonely, but now I'm sort of regretting it." I shake my head. "Won't she feel even lonelier when we talk about our memories? Sometimes my mouth opens before my brain thinks."

"Well, your heart is open, that's for sure. One of the things I'm coming to love about you."

Did he use the L word? Does it also surprise him because he looks away with a slight smile on his face, as if he slipped up.

I reach up and pull his face toward mine so I can gaze at his eyes. "I've had a couple of nights of good sleep and I've come to some conclusions."

"You have?" His eyebrows furrow.

"I have. Been thinking of us. . . our friendship. . .or whatever this thing we have is. Yes, one could say friendship. In our case it's. . .well…let's say it's both silver and gold."

"How's that?"

"We're new friends, so to speak, but we go way back. And that's gold."

He wraps his arms around me so tightly he almost lifts me off the ground. "Okay, golden girl, how about some lunch?"

Pulling cold cuts out of the fridge, I say. "Like I said before, I'm having second thoughts about inviting JoAnna."

"Why is that?"

"I can't quite put my finger on it, but somehow whenever she's around, the conversation seems to take a turn to some kind of foreboding. Not so much an Eeyore-kind of dark cloud but something almost sinister. Creepy, huh?"

"Yeah, kind of."

"There's one good thing about her. She volunteered to bring all the goodies for S'mores."

"So now I suppose you want me to be a good Boy Scout and sharpen four long sticks for you too."

"Nope. JoAnna said she found some nice steel prongs, especially for s'mores, with sharp ends, so you're off the hook."

"Sounds like I'm off the hook, but the marshmallows aren't."

"That's a terrible pun." I roll my eyes.

"Couldn't resist," he says as he picks up his notebook. "Let's do our recap."

We began a weekly ritual of making a list of what went well and not so well during the week. Left column: Big hits. Right column: Never again.

While slathering butter on four slices of bread for grilled cheese sandwiches, I say,

"The firefly competition was fun. Who could capture the most. When you're in town you might pick up more mason jars. But do you think the boys would like catching the fireflies as much as the girls did?"

Paul says, "They'll like the lawn games we did 4th of July week better. Tug- of -war, the egg toss, the water balloons. Should be even more fun with boys who love to get wet. Raw eggs, slimier the better."

I load the bread up with generous slices of ham and cheese. "Think there's any cooked bacon around here? It would give these sandwiches a little more pizzazz. I'm a firm believer that bacon makes everything better."

Paul opens the refrigerator door and slides open a few trays.

"That's for sure. Butter and bacon. Two of my favorites, but we're out of luck. Edna and Mabel left this place spotless. We should be getting a food delivery today."

I say, "Most boys like anything competitive. Especially if there's a prize involved. Like canteen coupons." I place the sandwiches in a skillet. "Under the Never Again column, if we have swim-relay races, we should make sure all the kids can swim. Little Rosie swallowed a gallon of pool water before we discovered she couldn't."

I flip the sandwiches. "Mari said sharks and minnows was a big hit in the pool."

After polishing off the grilled ham and cheese sandwiches, Paul closes his notebook and looks at me. "Have I told you lately how glad I am you're here this summer?" He covers my hand with his.

"You may have mentioned it a few times." I cover his hand with mine and then we start the slap, slap, one hand over the other and break up laughing.

He opens his notebook again. "Just for the record, we need to do a more personal recap of the week." He flips to a clean page and draws a line down the middle. At the top of the left column, he writes in caps. THINGS THAT WENT WELL WITH KIM THIS WEEK—MUST REPEAT. In the right-hand column, he prints, DON'T TRY THAT AGAIN with a little frown face. ☹

On the left side he writes, Swinging on the porch after lights out. "Would you like to add to it?" He slides the notebook to me.

Instead of writing, I say, "It's not about us, but I do like how you always take time to listen to the campers when they come to you. Even when they interrupt something you're doing, you act like you have all the time in the world."

"Who can resist a group of cute giggling girls?"

"Some of them this last week had a little crush on you. I remember my last summer as a camper. I had a huge crush on the lifeguard. Me and every other girl. Can't remember his name but can picture him on his lofty perch with his sunglasses, sun-bleached blond hair and dark tan."

"Hey, this is supposed to be about us. Not your past loves."

"Hardly love, but it sure made swimming more interesting."

"Was Mike your first love?"

"First and only. Maybe that's why the divorce was so painful."

"Would you say you're over it?"

"I'm over Mike, but the divorce still hurts at times. I see it as a personal failure. I grew up thinking 'happily ever after' and all that, and often ask myself if I could have prevented it." I shrug. "How about you and your southern belle? Thoughts of her often?"

"Occasionally, but not once this summer. Found someone better to think about."

"Hey, I just had a thought. Now that I know about AA, I bet your little lady might have wanted more mint juleps on the plantation patio than you were willing to partake."

He smiles at me. "Don't change the subject, Kim. You're what I think about, and I do think about you a lot. A very wise person told me once that you know when you're in—well, when you really care about someone—if you think about them all the time when you aren't with them, then that proves you're really supposed to be with them."

A warmth spreads through me. Did he almost use the L word again? "I think about you too. Also a lot."

He closes the notebook. "Let's stop thinking so much and do what we tell our little campers to do after lunch."

I grin and wait for his suggestion.

"We say, 'Go to your cabins and have a quiet rest time. Maybe even a little nap.'"

He takes my hand and we walk to his cabin.

How Does Your Garden Grow?

The boys' counselors start arriving about two for their orientation with Paul. I go back to the kitchen to check on snacks and drinks for Trish and Lois. I also pull out the old camp scrapbooks for them to look at. Thumbing through them, memories flood back in. The fun camp songs we sang like the silly John Jacob Jingleheimer Schmidt. I smile. The evening usually ended with a big group hug or Kumbaya.

Then a strange and vivid memory takes shape in my mind. We ten-year old campers were all in the group hug, but one of our cabin mates was not. She hung back. Still after all these years, I remember the expression on her pudgy face. It wasn't sadness that she wasn't included; it looked more like anger. Then I remember our counselor saying, "Pat, come join us. Come in the circle."

I remember the girl cautiously inched toward the circle when several of the girls broke the chain of hands and ran to the cabin door before she could be a part of the symbolic joining of friendship. Thinking of that moment now as an adult, I sense how cruel that was. Was I a part of the cruelty? I don't remember running, but I do remember lying in the bunk next to Pat that night and hearing her muffled sobs.

With thoughts of lonely people, I turn to JoAnna once again. I never did ask her the questions I meant to about her past, the questions that were raised when I accidentally read her school records and resume in the director's file. Why wouldn't she go by the name on all her school records—Patricia?

What a weird coincidence it was that I was thinking of two Pat's, or one Pat and one Patricia. Pat the Camper and Patricia the Nurse.

I turn to see Emma running up the front porch steps with yet another Nancy Drew mystery in her hands. "So what great mystery is Nancy solving this time?" I ask her, always enjoying Emma's enthusiasm to share the latest adventure. She does not disappoint.

"It's a good one. Someone tries to poison someone using a common household product. Can you guess what it is?" Emma likes testing me since I told her I read all the Nancy Drew books. "Let me think a minute," I say "Would it be insecticide? It's poisonous and most people have it in their homes."

Emma shakes her head with a smile, enjoying our little game.

I say, "How about arsenic? That's how the old spinster aunts in the movie, Arsenic and Old Lace, killed lonely old men. Served them homemade wine, if I recall, that had arsenic in it. It's a very old movie. Probably way before your time, but your grandpa might remember it."

"Wow, that sounds like a good story," Emma said. "You're getting close, but it's not the right answer. Do you give up?"

"I do."

'Remember I said it was common?"

"Yes."

"It's also something no one would suspect. Would you ever believe a beautiful flower would be poisonous?"

"No, not really. I know mushrooms can be, but they're not pretty."

Emma laughed. "It's a flower called Foxglove. Nancy discovers it in the victim's garden. The killer used the victim's own flower to try to kill her. Not the flower but the seeds of the flower. That was pretty clever."

"It certainly was." The mention of that flower triggers a thought, but I can't quite place it.

"If I were going to commit a murder, I would choose something like that—something that seems innocent but isn't." Emma heads downstairs. "Mr. Paul said I could have something from the canteen since I helped him count all the candy before the boys arrived."

I pass through the dining room on my way out and see the centerpieces on each table. They need to be cleared off before the boys come. Definitely not their thing. Especially paper flowers the girls made on craft night.

Flowers. That little something that was nagging on my brain comes to the front. JoAnna bought foxglove at the nursery. Was there a reason she chose that flower? Once again, her actions raise doubts in my mind.

The Big Chill

Trish and Lois arrive together promptly at three o'clock. They unload the car with enough supplies for days.

I laugh. "I'm so glad to see you, but really, this is just one overnight."

Lois says, "Boy Scouts aren't the only ones with the 'Be Prepared' motto." She lifts out two bottles of red wine. "I'm going to make my signature sangria for poolside relaxation."

Trish is carrying two sacks of groceries. "My signature piece is one-pot pasta. Start to finish—twenty minutes."

"Shortcut to the kitchen," I say and lead them to the back entrance.

"Is anyone here besides us?" Lois asks.

"All the counselors and staff are gone for the weekend. Even the cooks took off. Of course Herb is always here."

"Herb is still here? Oh my goodness. He seemed old when we were here. I'd love to see him," Lois says.

"We could arrange that. His wife passed away, but he has two adorable granddaughters who spend a lot of time here with him. I'm sure little Emma will surface with her nose in a book. Tomorrow the boys arrive. This will be totally new for me. They tell me all that rampant testosterone requires a whole new energy level. I'm doubling up on my vitamins."

"Speaking of boys—or should I say—big boys, where's that cute camp director? Did you run him off too?" Lois asks.

"No, he's here. Training new counselors now, but he'll be around this evening and spend the night here. He did promise to stay out of our sight. Unless we need him to ward off the scary camp monsters that lurk in the woods."

"Do they still talk about Crazy Man Wilson?" Lois asks.

"Oh, sure, he's a legend. Especially with the boys, I'm told."

Trish says, "Do we get to walk to the clearing? And sit around the campfire?"

"Of course. I invited JoAnna, the camp nurse, to join us for dinner and campfire. Hope you don't mind. She spends most weekends here and seems so lonely."

"You haven't changed a bit. It's a good thing you don't work at the animal shelter. You would take every mangy dog home."

"So, what's first? Drinks and munchies poolside?" Lois asks.

"Sounds good." I open cupboards and drawers in the kitchen to show them where supplies are.

Trish whips up a plate of veggies and hummus and Lois throws orange and apple slices into a pitcher. She mashes them with a wooden spatula. Adds in some brown sugar and gives it a generous pour of rum before she pours orange juice and a bottle of red wine. She stirs, adds a few ice cubes, she says, "Voilà!"

"Okay, Trish, your hummus looks delicious," Lois comments, "but way too healthy. If we're going back in time, we need all the junk food we ate then." She digs into a sack that looks like a Mary Poppins carpet bag with an endless bottom and brings out bags of corn chips, a jar of con queso dip, a package of dried salami slices, and a jar of peanuts. "See? Now we have all three food essentials—protein, carbs, and fats."

"You haven't changed either, Lois. And that's a good thing," Trish says and dunks a chip into the dip.

"Grab your suits and change in my cabin."

We change into our suits and carry the tray of food, drinks and plastic cups to the pool. A perfect clear summer day. Sunny but not too hot. We decide to take a dip first and then lay out.

The main topic of conversation is our favorite camp memories. I say, "We can't sleep in our old cabin but we can stay in the tent as JoAnna suggested. Or Pottawatami II, one of the craft cabins now converted."

"I vote for the cabin." Trish says, "Even a cot is better than the damp ground."

"Oh, yeah, crafts. Can we make some lanyards? I can take them home for my kids," Lois says.

I offer to bring the lanyard supplies to the pool so we can keep enjoying our refreshments and sangria with an occasional dip.

After pool time, we change our clothes and visit the camp store, and I invite them to pick out a camp souvenir of days gone by. My treat. Lois chooses a camp nightie and Trish takes a GAC sweatshirt. We head downstairs and they belly up to the canteen like they used to, having to make major decisions, like choosing between a candy necklace and a long rope of licorice. The bowling pins are all set up, so we bowl a few lines, and Trish challenges Lois to a ping-pong match.

"I love this," Trish says. "I feel like a kid again."

We return to the big Lodge kitchen and start whipping up dinner. Lois chops salad greens and Trish throws all her ingredients into a huge pot—sausage, onions, tomatoes, mushrooms, garlic, a splash of olive oil, pasta and chicken broth—and stirs it up. "So easy," she says. All in one pot…no draining….no sticky pasta. Done in twenty minutes."

Lois opens the other bottle of wine that didn't go in the sangria. "I don't suppose there's any fancy wine glasses in this kid-friendly kitchen," she says as she opens cupboard drawers. "Juice glasses. Perfect."

I set my I-Pod and speaker on the island in the middle of the kitchen, and "Can't Stop the Music" by Rihanna blares out. We start moving around to the beat and next thing we are full-fledge dancing to the music.

Trish says, "Hey, I watched an old DVD last week of The Big Chill. Remember that? The dance scene in the kitchen while they're cooking. I loved it."

Lois says, "I remember that. Great movie about old friends. Like us now." She raises her juice glass and Kim and Trish do the same. Lois starts singing off-key, I've Got Sunshine on a Cloudy Day. "Every time I hear that I think of our summer here."

"This girl time is good for my soul," I tell them. "I haven't had this since my breakup with Mike. Let's plan to get together again—" I notice JoAnna standing at the kitchen entry, watching us with a weird expression on her face.

Tag-a-long

JoAnna joins us for dinner and I try to sway the conversation to our current lives so as not to make her feel left out.

After dinner and cleanup, we relax on the front porch waiting for darkness to begin our walk through the woods to the clearing site and campfire. A few fireflies are coming out, and we recall how we ran up and down the front lawn capturing them in mason jars with holes punched in the lids.

Just as we're about to leave the Lodge, Emma comes running up the front porch stairs. "There you are, Miss Kim." She holds up a Nancy Drew book. "I started The Mystery at Lilac Inn."

I introduce her to Lois and Trish. "These were my friends when I was a camper. And you know Nurse JoAnna."

She gives Lois and Trish the once-over. "Wow. You're still friends? That was a long time ago, wasn't it?"

Lois laughs. "Nothing like a kid's honesty, brutal as it can be."

I say to Emma, "It was a long time ago, but we thought it would be fun to relive some of those special times. We're walking down to the campfire tonight. And we're going to have s'mores."

Her eyes open wide. "Smores? Can I come?"

"I don't see why not. As long as it's okay with your grandfather."

"Oh, thank you, Miss Kim. I'll go ask him. He's waiting for me in the truck. He gave me a ride here so I could show you my new book."

"Okay, we'll wait here on the front porch."

JoAnna seems ruffled. "Do you really think she should tag along? You know it could be late."

"I'll leave that up to her grandfather. I couldn't say no with the way her eyes lit up."

Emma comes bounding back up the steps. "He said yes."

We go toward the path, walking silently in single file with our flashlights shining ahead of us. I lead the way and Emma is close behind me. Trish and Lois are carrying blankets. JoAnna has the container with all the s'more supplies.

Besides my little pocket flashlight, I'm carrying a big one Paul gave me with a high beam. There's a full moon, so it's not as pitch black as some of the Friday nights we walked. Paul has arranged the logs in a little square close to the pit. We spread the blankets on the logs to avoid splinters in our bottoms.

"Let's get this fire crackling, and then we'll get a little assembly line going." I caution Emma to stand back as I strike a match and throw it into the pile of paper and twigs.

Whoosh. It flames.

"What is it about a fire that is so mesmerizing?" Trish says, "Even without the promise of a s'more, it seems to capture us."

Lois says, "I agree but I'd like to capture some of that gooey goodness. My thanks to whoever came up with this idea in the first place."

"Well, funny you should ask." I reply, "I did some research on that very subject the other day."

"Really? Wow, I'm impressed," Trish says.

"I'm writing an article about camp experiences. Too late for this summer, but I'll pitch it to Parents Magazine for next year."

Lois says, "So tell us, who made the first s'more? Surely not cavemen. They could hardly go to Kroger's for a bag of marshmallows."

"No one agrees on how s'mores originated or how they got their silly name. But many agree it could have only been invented by a kid. Nobody over ten years old would ever think of squishing together a chocolate bar and toasted marshmallow between a pair of graham crackers and calling it food."

The fire crackles and I go on. "As early as 1927, there was a recipe in a Girl Scout magazine. Other sources attribute it to the Campfire Girls."

JoAnna lines up four long spears in a row. Emma counts them and looks concerned.

I say to her, "You and I can share." I continue, "According to period newspaper reports of 1892, marshmallow roasts were the latest in summer fads. The article said the proper means of consuming marshmallows is to nibble them directly off the end of the stick—or off the end of your neighbor's stick. It was called an 'excellent medium for flirtation.'"

Lois says, "Let's stop flirting with them and start roasting them."

JoAnna smiles. "Yes, let's get on with this." She hands Trish a package of graham crackers. "Do you want to break these in half?" Then she gives Lois the chocolate bars. "You can put pieces between the graham crackers."

"You trust me with all this chocolate? You really shouldn't," she says, as she breaks off a piece and pops it in her mouth. "Quality control. Making sure no one has poisoned them." She laughs.

"Oh, I don't think you have to worry about the chocolate." JoAnna reaches for the marshmallows.

The Big Spill

"I love marshmallows," Emma exclaims, "Can I have some just plain before we do the s'mores?" She doesn't wait for an answer but jumps up and tears the bag open, not realizing it's already unsealed. With a tug, all the marshmallows fall out and land right into the fire.

"Oh, no. I spilled them all." Emma starts crying.

"You stupid, clumsy girl," JoAnna shrieks.

I glare at JoAnna. "It's no big deal. We have another bag, don't we?"

"I'm sorry," Emma says between sobs.

I put my arms around her. "Honey, it's okay."

"I told you we shouldn't have let her come. Now everything is ruined," JoAnna says.

Lois says, "Well, I wouldn't say everything is ruined. Don't we have another bag?"

"That was a special bag. A very special bag." JoAnna's tone is fierce.

"Special? In what way?" Trish stares at her.

Even in the dim glow of the fire, the look in JoAnna's eyes sends a chill through me. What is she talking about? Special marshmallows?

I try to salvage the occasion. "We can still melt the chocolate between the crackers, can't we?"

JoAnna looks at me with a smirk. "So how are we supposed to get a cracker on the fork?"

Lois says, "Yeah, that could be a little tricky."

Emma's shoulders quake. "I'm sorry, Miss Kim."

The burnt sugary smell of marshmallows fills the air. We seem hypnotized by the charred remains until a sudden movement to my side catches my attention. Right before our eyes, JoAnna rams the sharp end of one of the metal prongs into Trish's upper arm.

Blood spurts out. Trish screams.

JoAnna shrieks, "Take that, you big-mouthed bitch. Telling the whole camp my shorts were bigger than the tent."

Emma screams.

I stand there frozen, and then JoAnna whips around and rams the spear into Lois's side.

Lois screams and I lunge at JoAnna, knocking her down. The back of her head hits the log, but she's waving the spear like a mad woman, just missing my face.

I manage to straddle her and pin both wrists down. Then I twist her right wrist as hard as I can until she drops the spear.

My brain is racing. Where's my phone? "Emma. Get help. Take the big flashlight. Run as fast as you can to Mr. Paul. Think of what Nancy Drew would do. Can you be brave like her?"

"Yes, I can." Emma grabs the flashlight and runs.

I shout to her. "Tell Mr. Paul to call 911 quick. Tell him there's blood. Now. Run, Nancy, run."

I need to help Trish and Lois, but I don't want to get off of JoAnna. I don't know what else she is capable of doing. JoAnna's pushing hard against me, trying to throw me off. She seems to have supernatural strength.

Trish, with her left arm bleeding, gets up and with her right hand grabs one of the spears by the pointy end. She brings the other end of the spear, the wooden handle, down hard on JoAnna's head. JoAnna screams and loosens her grip on me. Trish turns the stick around so the prongs are almost touching JoAnna's face. "If you move so much as an inch, I'm putting this fork right in your face, hear me?"

I jump off of JoAnna and rush to Lois who is bleeding profusely from her side. I rip off my tee shirt and try to stuff it in the wound, pressing down around it to staunch the bleeding if I can. "Hang in there, Lois. Help is on the way."

JoAnna is crying and muttering, "It was supposed to be the perfect ending. The final revenge. The end of all the pain I've endured."

"What are you talking about," I ask her. "What pain?"

"Let me refresh your memory. Pottawatami cabin. 1987. Hearing the other campers say, Pat, Pat, she's so fat. Made a dent in the bed where she sat. Or my other nickname, Pee Pee Pat. And the snake in my bed. How would you like to feel something slithering in your pajamas?"

"But you said you were never a camper here. I'm confused."

"JoAnna Parsons was never a camper, but Patty Jo Mann was. Mann was my maiden name. When I married, I used my middle name and added the Anna. After my divorce I kept the name. I wanted to start over. Patty Jo Mann was a frightened person."

Oh, and this psychotic person is better?

"You weren't as bad as the others, Kim. I probably wouldn't have hunted you down to get my revenge, but since you came to me, it was just too easy. Too tempting. And even though you never started the taunts, you never told them to stop, so in a way, you were just as guilty as they were." She stifles a sob. "Seeing you laugh this weekend with your counselor friends reminded me of all of you again having fun. Sometimes at my expense. So tight, so close, and so mean to leave me out."

JoAnna squirms again to evade the poker Trish is pointing at her. Trish prods the poker lightly into her neck and JoAnna whimpers.

"It would have worked so well if that little brat hadn't dumped the whole bag."

"So what was so special about the marshmallows anyway?"

"Oh, just an added touch injected. Handy to have needles and syringes. A few ground seeds of foxglove." JoAnna sounds proud of herself. "Actually quite a few. Quite poisonous. Quick acting too."

"You were going to poison little innocent Emma, too?" I ask in disbelief.

"No, I wouldn't have let her have one of the bad ones. I did have another bag. Untouched. I'm not a monster, you know."

"So you weren't going to kill Emma? You were just going to let her watch other people die?"

I think of Wendy and Sara. Is she the monster that caused their deaths? Time to talk with the police.

Paul runs into the clearing. "What in the world—?" He surveys the scene. Trish, her arm still bleeding, stands with a fork over JoAnna's face. Me, in just my bra, stuffing my shirt into Lois' wound.

Paul takes his jacket off and wraps it around my shoulders. "Here, put this on," he says. "I'll tend to this wound."

Lois is moaning but still conscious. He presses down on the tee shirt with his left hand and feels her wrist with his right hand. "Her pulse is strong, but I'm sure she's in shock."

The sound of an ambulance in the distance gets louder.

"Will the medics know how to reach the clearing?" I ask.

"One of the counselors is watching for them. He'll lead them down."

Emma has followed Paul back and is standing there crying. "This is all my fault. I spilled the marshmallows."

Paul says, "All this over a bag of marsh—?"

Two paramedics burst into the clearing carrying a gurney and a third one follows with a box of medical supplies. They flip open the box and pull out gauze pads to pack the wound. "Quick, get some fluids in her."

They gently lift Lois unto the gurney and insert a needle into her arm for the IV. "We need to get her to the hospital now."

"Wait, how about Trish?" I ask, as I point to her arm, but it appears the bleeding has stopped.

The third paramedic examines her arm further, cleans the wound and wraps it. "This might require stitches. Can you walk?"

Trish nods. I take the prong from her and keep it pointed at JoAnna's face.

The paramedic turns and says to me, "The sheriff should be here any minute. All 911 calls go out to both of us."

As he says this, the sheriff, a bit overweight and huffing, appears in the clearing and surveys the area. "So, what do we have here?" he asks.

"That's exactly what I would like to know," Paul says.

Emma is still sobbing softly. I hand Paul the prong and take her in my arms. "You were such a brave girl tonight. I think you saved all our lives."

"Really?" she asks, her red eyes wide.

"Really," I say. "Paul, would you please take Emma to her grandfather's house while I explain to the sheriff what happened here tonight?"

I turn to Emma. "You get some good sleep tonight and don't worry about anything. None of this is your fault. We'll talk about it tomorrow. We'll call it 'The Mystery of the S'mores.'"

Through her tears a glimmer of a little smile appears at the thought of delving into another mystery. "Okay, Miss Kim." She takes Paul's hand and they walk toward the path.

I point the prong at JoAnna and say to the sheriff, "You might want to restrain this woman. She attempted to poison us and stabbed two women."

"Well if that doesn't beat all." The sheriff shakes his head and pulls out his handcuffs.

"When you have more time, pull up a log and I'll tell you a campfire story you may not believe."

Bullies

While the sheriff walks JoAnna to her cabin to get a few belongings before he takes her to the station, Paul and I ride to the hospital to check on Trish and Lois. Trish's cut is stitched up and she is released to us. Fortunately, Lois suffers no internal damage but they are keeping her overnight.

In spite of her injury, Lois seems chipper. "Some party you throw, Kim. A little low on refreshments. I never did get that s'more."

"Be thankful for that," I say. "Were you conscious when JoAnna told what she did to the marshmallows?"

"Sort of, but refresh my memory, please. Is it a recipe I'm going to want?"

"Hardly. Time-consuming and labor-intensive, I imagine." I hold up one finger. "Step One: Buy flowers that contain poisonous seeds. Two. Crush seeds to a pulp. Three. Add enough water to liquefy. Four. Fill syringes and inject into marshmallows. Five. Roast marshmallows and place between chocolate and graham cracker. Six. Serve to trusting friends, preferably around a remote campfire in the woods."

"Wow. That took some planning."

"Yes, like twenty-some years."

"I've counseled some disturbed people through the years, but this one has to be—" Lois' voice trails off.

"Try to get some sleep. Your hubby's on the way to stay with you tonight."

Lois blinks her eyes and sounds wistful, "I was looking forward to sleeping under the stars tonight, not looking at this." She nods to an IV stand dripping saline solution into her arm.

"Remote as we were, the paramedics got there quickly, thanks to little Emma's fast run. We'll talk more later."

Paul, Trish and I return to the campground. The light is on at Herb's so we stop in to see how Emma is doing. She's in her pajamas sitting at the kitchen table with Herb, drinking what looks like a mug of hot chocolate. She jumps up when she sees us.

"Miss Kim, I was trying to explain to Grandpa what happened tonight, but I don't know why Miss JoAnna was so angry."

Herb says, "Please sit. Tell me how this all came about."

"Emma, do they ever talk about bullies at your school?" I say.

"Yes, we are not supposed to bully anyone."

"That's right. Bullying is not right. And making fun of other people is sort of like bullying. It hurts a lot."

Emma nods.

"Well, a long time ago, Miss JoAnna was a camper. Right here. She was a camper in Pottawatomi. Some of the other campers made fun of her. She was fat and they did some mean things like call her names, and one night they put a snake in her bed."

"Yikes. A snake in her bed? That was really mean." Emma says.

"Yes, it was. And Miss JoAnna kept thinking about those things. Even after she grew up. The more she thought about them, the madder she got. And then she wanted to hurt the girls who hurt her."

"Why didn't she just tell the mean girls to stop being mean? Or why didn't someone else tell the mean girls to stop it. At school they tell us that if we see someone being mean, we should tell the teacher."

"You are so right, Emma. Even if we're not the bully, if we stand by and do nothing, we're just as bad." I pat the top of her head and get up to leave. "Good-night, Herb. You have a brave little granddaughter."

As we walk to our respective cabins, Paul says, "Do you want to sit on the swing for a while? Need to unwind?"

"That might be nice for a few minutes. It's going to be a short night. The boys will be arriving in less than eight hours."

We swing silently. Other than an occasional creak of the swing, the night is still.

Paul says, "You're awful quiet. Are you alright?"

"It's this revenge thing. Thinking how at one time I wanted to hurt Mike as he hurt me. Now I'm so thankful that feeling passed once I told him how I felt."

Paul says, "I take it JoAnna never got to tell anyone how she was mistreated.

"I'm thinking about what Emma said too. She's right. Even though I didn't make fun of JoAnna, or Pat, as she was called then, I did nothing to stop it. I'm just as guilty."

Paul rubs the top of my head, "Hey, don't be so hard on yourself. What were you? Nine or ten years old?"

I look at him and am reminded of what a kind person he is. He cups my face in his hand, "Have I told you lately—"

"You're still glad I'm here? After my horrendous reunion?"

"Still glad." He kisses me gently. "Let's get some sleep and be ready to give those seven and eight-year old boys a week they'll always remember."

August 2010

Paul was able to replace nurse JoAnna by the end of the first boys' week and appropriately with a male nurse, Henry, who turned out to be a great umpire for the baseball games played each night after dinner. Impressed the boys with his knuckle-ball pitch.

The weeks passed with no major calamities other than more roughhousing in the pool, playing King of the Mountain and Chicken. A near miss concussion when one toppled over too close to the edge of the pool. Only fifteen stitches and one broken bone in the five weeks. A few cases of poison ivy. Not bad for a summer of adventurous daring boys.

Mabel continued to dish out versions of scriptures with scrambled eggs. Her morning favorite was 1 Corinthians 10:31. ...whatever you do, do all to the Glory of God.

Lucy seemed to resign herself to the idea that Paul and I might be an item and stopped approaching him at every opportunity.

At the close of camp for the summer, the usual good-byes were heard in the parking lot as counselors and staff departed.

"Email me when you get to college. "I'll come back next year if you do."

Lots of hugs, some tears, and even the guys were seen doing the man-hug thing.

Before everyone takes off, Paul says one last time over the loud speaker, "Meet on the front lawn for group photo." Then the strains of Bob Hope singing "Thanks for the Memories" can be heard throughout the campground.

As the last car pulls away, Paul and I stand side-by-side with our arms around each other. We give each other the usual high-five but this time there's a touch of sadness rather than celebration.

"Guess I better pack up too," I say.

"Meet you on the porch swing tonight when you're done?" Paul asks.

All Good Things Must End

We swing silently for a while and then Paul states the obvious, "I'll be heading back to Arizona in a few days."

"And I'll be heading back to Chicago." I look out toward the sky. "Trading starry nights for city lights. Let's get out from under the porch and look at those beautiful stars one last time."

We lay on the grassy hill side by side and look up. The stars are extra bright with no moon or city lights to dim them.

"I'm going to miss this," I say.

"I'm going to miss you." Paul takes my hand in his, intertwining his fingers in mine.

"Why don't you come to Arizona for a visit before you get back to your Chicago routine?"

"Arizona in August? I've heard it's a bit toasty. What am I ? A martyr? Or is this a test of our relationship?"

"No, you passed that test a long time ago." Paul turns on his side, leans up on one elbow and looks down at me. "Maybe as far back as high school. Standing over that frog when I thought you were going to be sick. I wanted to protect you even then."

"Yes, you were my gallant knight to the rescue with your trusty scalpel."

"Would a fair maiden give her gallant knight a kiss under the stars?"

I laugh.

"What?" Paul sits up. "What a mood breaker you are."

"Sorry, I'm remembering what my sister said the first time I told her about meeting you again."

"So what did she say that was so funny? Something like 'You're going to spend the summer with that nerdy kid?'"

"No, silly, she said I might have to kiss a lot of frogs to find my prince again."

Paul smiles. "Frogs, princes, knights. Whatever. Can we just kiss?"

And so we did.

An Ariel View

If one were to fly over Good Acres that final Saturday of camp, one would see that the kitchen has been scrubbed down, stainless steel appliances gleaming and ready for the next summer.

The pool waters are still and ready to be drained, although Herb promised the maintenance crew one last evening swim when they're done cleaning out the cabins. All the remaining arts and craft supplies are stowed in the Lodge closet. The canteen shelves are devoid of candy necklaces, and the ice-cream freezer has been emptied. The ping-pong and Foosball tables are silenced.

At Herb's house, one would see Kim giving Emma a good-bye hug and handing her something. If our aerial view permitted sound waves to travel upward, we would hear Kim say, "Emma, here's a book you might like."

"Is it a mystery?"

"No, it's a true story. A diary. Remember we talked about the diary we found that Nurse JoAnna kept when she was a camper. How she wrote down all the mean things the other girls said to her?"

Emma says, "Yes, I remember." She hesitates with a little frown and looks down at the book. "I'm not sure I want to read a diary."

Kim says, "Not all diaries are bad. The girl who wrote this one is thirteen, so you might want to wait a few years to read it. But I want you to have it because even though she talks about some bad things people do, in the end, she still believes that most people are good."

Kim hands Emma The Diary of Anne Frank.

EPILOGUE
Summer 2020

Paul and I drive to Good Acres campground on Sunday morning and get in line with the rest of the cars waiting for the gate to open promptly at noon. Our nine-year-old daughter, Leslie, is bouncing up and down in the back seat. Her seven-year old brother beside her is playing a game on an I-Pad.

Leslie can hardly contain herself and chatters incessantly. "I can't wait to get in. Last year was so much fun. I wonder what cabin I'll be in. I hope I like my cabinmates. I'm going swimming first thing this afternoon. I'm going to make the longest lanyard anyone ever made. Will the cooks make those cinnamon buns again? They were so good."

Paul looks at me. "Guess we don't have to worry about anyone getting homesick, do we?"

I smile. "As they say, she's one happy camper."

In the car behind them, a little girl has her head bent down in the back seat and is writing something in her diary. I hate camp. I wish I didn't have to come back again. Last year the other girls were so mean.

THE END

Author's Note to Reader:

Thank you for choosing to read my book. If you enjoyed it, would you please refer to friends? Word-of-mouth is the best compliment I could hope for. I'm shamelessly asking for your endorsement. ☺

Also, if you would be so kind to refer it to people you may not even know by posting a review on Amazon.

It's easy. Just find the book on Amazon, click on the cover image and a screen will appear with book title and stars under it. Click on the stars and on the left side will appear a link to write a review. Can be just a few words and you can also fill in the number of stars you think it deserves 1-5. I thank you in advance by including some recipes below.

My other books are also available on Amazon: I'll Always Be With You, Still With You, and A Mahjongg Mystery. Recipes from the first books are on my website: www.violettaarmour.com

Trish's One-Pot Pasta

Essentially the idea is that you don't have to pre-cook the pasta. The pasta cooks with the sauce and vegetables all together in one pan. It's one less pan you have to use, which means quicker dinner on the table and quicker cleanup. And it's delicious--every time I serve this, people want the recipe!

Ingredients

- 8 ounces linguine or regular spaghetti
- 1 lb. Italian sausage (can omit for vegetarian dish)
- 1 pint cherry tomatoes sliced in half (or a can of diced tomatoes)
- 2 ounces baby spinach leaves
- 1 small onion finely sliced
- 3 garlic cloves finely sliced
- A small handful of basil leaves roughly chopped
- 2 tablespoons extra virgin olive oil
- 1/2 teaspoon crushed red pepper
- 1/2 teaspoon salt
- 2 ounces parmesan cheese grated (optional)

Instructions

In a large deep pan, brown the sausage. Then place the linguine in addition to the cherry tomatoes, spinach, sliced onions, garlic and basil. Drizzle the olive oil on top and season with crushed red pepper and salt.

Pour 4 cups of hot chicken stock into the pan and bring the mixture to a boil. Cook for 8-10 minutes on medium heat stirring occasionally with tongs to push all the pasta deep into the pan, until the liquid is nearly evaporated, creating a sauce.

Remove the pan from heat and stir in parmesan cheese and fresh basil, if desired. Serve immediately and enjoy warm.

Lois' Sangria

1/2 medium apple (cored, skin on, chopped into small pieces)

1/2 medium orange (rind on, sliced into small pieces, large seeds removed // plus more for garnish)

3-4 Tbsp brown sugar

3/4 cup orange juice (plus more to taste)

1/3 cup rum (plus more to taste)

1 bottle dry red wine

1 cup ice to chill

Instructions

1. Add apples, oranges, and sugar to a large pitcher and muddle with a muddler or wooden spoon for 45 seconds.
2. Add orange juice and rum and muddle again for 30 seconds to get rum flavor into the fruit.
3. Add red wine and stir to incorporate, then taste and adjust flavor as needed. I added a bit more rum, orange juice and brown sugar. Stir to combine.
4. Add ice and stir once more to chill. Serve as is, or with a bit more ice. Garnish with orange segments (optional).
5. Best served in a glass pitcher to see all colorful fruits, unless you are poolside. Use plastic pitcher.
6. Store leftovers covered in the refrigerator for up to 48 hours, though best when fresh.

Edna's Secret Ingredient Sloppy Joes

Recipe reduced from industrial size to serve 6-8.

1 lb. ground beef and 1 lb. ground pork (or 2 lbs. ground beef)
1 onion finely diced
2 Tablespoons oil
½ cup brown sugar
1 Tablespoon mustard
1 cup ketchup
1 Tablespoon dill pickle relish
Dash of Worchester sauce
Salt and pepper to taste
Secret Ingredient: A splash of regular Coco-Cola (not diet)

Saute onion in oil until transparent (in pan large enough for 2 lbs. meat). Set onions aside.

In same pan, brown both meat mixtures and crush into small pieces as you brown.

Remove excess grease from the meat and combine with onion into original pan.

Add rest of ingredients and simmer for 20-30 minutes to a good consistency, reducing sauce.

Serve on buns, plain or toasted. (Toasted is best).

Pickles and cheese slices on bun are optional.

S'mores

8 sheets honey graham crackers
One 4.4-ounce bar milk chocolate, such as Hershey's, broken into 4 pieces

8 large marshmallows

1. Heat a grill to medium-low heat. The heat coming from a dying charcoal grill or a gas grill cooling down will also work well. Or ideally, from an outdoor campfire.
2. Halve each graham cracker sheet crosswise into 2 squares.
3. Working with 1 or 2 s'mores at a time, place a square of graham cracker on a piece of foil and top with a portion of chocolate.
4. Working with a few at a time, skewer 2 marshmallows on a long fork or metal skewer and hold over the heat about 2 inches above the grates or outdoor fire flame. Toast, turning occasionally, until the marshmallow puffs and turns golden brown, 1 to 2 minutes.
5. Using the square of graham with the chocolate and a plain graham square, place the marshmallow on the chocolate and, using the plain graham, squish the marshmallow down and pull off the skewer. Eat while it is warm and gooey and perfect.

Creative crackers: Instead of plain graham crackers use:

Fudge Striped Cookies
Chocolate Covered Graham Cookie
Cinnamon Flavored Graham Cookie

Creative Filling:
Reese's peanut butter cups instead of plain chocolate (or both)

Violetta Armour lives in Sun Lakes, Arizona, where she enjoys the lifestyle an active retirement community offers. Her former careers include bookstore ownership, a national trainer for Better Homes and Gardens Real Estate, a Dale Carnegie instructor, and a high-school English teacher. Her current passions are playing pickleball, visiting bookclubs who select her books, attending writers' conferences and spoiling her grandchildren. Her debut novel, I'll Always Be With You has won several awards, followed by the sequel, Still With You. A Mah Jongg Mystery is the first in her Dangerous Pastime Series.

www.ingramcontent.com/pod-product-compliance
Lightning Source LLC
LaVergne TN
LVHW011813060526
838200LV00053B/3763